Scags at 30

Scags at 30

Deborah Emin

New York

Published by Sullivan Street Press, Inc., New York

Cover design by Patricia Rasch, interior design by Scribe

ISBN (digital) 9780996349116
ISBN (print) 9780997666328

This latest volume of the Scags series could not have been written without the love and support of my wife, Suzanne Pyrch.

Christmas, 1980

Hi there Lauren,

Here it is, Christmas in New York. Nothing is as we thought it would be when we said good-bye in August. But hey, that is the way life is—we both have moved on.

The city is aglow today with the lights and the excitement. I have mixed feelings about what all of this means and why I should care.

December 8, John Lennon was killed. The city went into paroxysms for a few days, as it would. I did too. I was shocked that someone could just walk up to him and shoot him and he would die. I was awake almost all night listening to the radio like thousands of other people. That voice at night, the radio voice, telling us we are together in times of tragedy—that can be such a comfort. And it highlighted for me how vulnerable we are.

We walk the streets and think our thoughts, happy to have been somewhere with friends or a lover, and then a shot rings out, its echoes careening through these canyons of brick walls, blood flowing into a small pool at our feet, life draining away as if we had been bitten by Dracula and there was no reversal of the Count's deed.

That sense of not being able to restore life after death consumed me for days. Then I learned from you that you had found a new lover, someone who was taking over my spot in your bed and heart. That came as a shock, because what I angrily thought of as your new love highlighted how duplicitous I have been.

So here's my confession. On this glorious night of Christmas, sitting with a full stomach and a warm heart for someone new, I can say this to you: I had hoped to have it both ways—to have you in Vermont and someone here, someone I am not sure can love me as you and I have loved, but someone I hope could be as true as you were.

My thought had been that if this living and loving in New York City didn't work out, I could come back to you. In my imagination, you were eagerly waiting for me to come home to you.

I had created this whole fantasy world of lovers. You were the central one. You were the lover I had assumed would never stray, and here it is, Christmas, and I am writing to you to say your news stung me even though, as I am confessing here, I have this new lover.

Yet, yet, yet . . . you know me so well. I am so afraid of this new life, of living here in a new city as a lesbian with a lover. I hated living in Vermont with you and being in the closet all the time and yet, yet, yet . . . you and I got along so well until we didn't.

I confess too, I never listen to you. I didn't pay attention to the letters you sent me. I ignored the details of the things you and Rose were doing together. How blind could I be? No one would write letters about someone making them dinners, keeping their dog entertained, or what a help this new person is when it comes to repairing the stove or fixing up a new room unless they were in love.

Where was I? What was I thinking? I must have thought, oh good, Lauren has a playmate and that will keep her busy until I return, if I return. You must have been so angry with me. I know I would have been.

I was so busy spinning my own tales for your benefit of what I was doing in the city—the walks to work in the shadow of the World Trade Center; the competing circles of friends I hooked into (my very own Kultur Klub and Artist Squatters); and the solo forays to museums, concerts, and poetry readings as I soaked up what I hoped could fill me up. And the fact is that all of this was a smokescreen for the one true thing I should have shared—that there was a new person in my life too.

Does this mean that I am now permanently living here? Does this mean that I am no longer from Vermont but from NYC? Damn, I am not sure that is what I want, but it is certainly where I am and how I am living, is it not?

Oh my, Lauren, I was so careless of you and your feelings.

I am certainly jealous of your new love. I know what it is like to live and be in love with you. We had seven years of that. And it was good until it was not enough.

How did I come to that realization? I know you asked me that question as I was packing to move here. I remember you standing in the doorway of the bedroom. It was August and hot in the midday sun. You had come home from work for lunch. I had forgotten to eat. You stood with a sandwich and a glass of water for me and waited for me to take it from you and to answer that question: What was I looking for?

I was so full of my own plans and how superior they were to anything going on in the present moment of our life together that I couldn't even be bothered to thank you for taking the time to make a sandwich for me.

In that moment, an insight also showed up on that plate you were holding. I was chasing after something so new and different because after many months, if not years, I could feel blood flowing through me, and it was not just warm but on fire.

Vermont and its homophobia were killing me. I could not breathe. I hated not being able to kiss you in public. I hated not being able to even hold hands during a movie.

The sad thing, though, is this: I arrived in New York City and realized almost at once that this place was not as open and kind as I had hoped it would be. In fact, at work, it is a danger to me and my own ambitions to be known as a lesbian. In fact, even my so-called enlightened friends are uncomfortable with any suggestion of homosexuality even though some of them are homosexuals.

This is a male-centric town too. Very much based on principles of hierarchy, where even if there were laws protecting women from abuse or harassment, they would be ignored and I would be a fool to try to accuse anyone of standing in my way due to my gender.

So the irony is clear. I walked away from you because I felt I would die of the homo-phobia all around us and came to this sup-posed magical city and found out just how difficult it is to be out here too.

My dreams of the two of us walking hand in hand through the Village and stopping for drinks and dancing could be true, but we would not be holding hands and we would not be kissing on the streets.

This Merry Christmas greeting is not in vain though. I have been celebrating what is possible right now with a new woman, one who has opened me to something else: a church and a group of people who are interested in creating a more open world where we can be free to kiss and hold hands.

I know these all sound like such flimsy tasks or goals, but when you want to be with someone, when you think you may be in love with the person you need to be with (once again, I am at that crossroad), how do you become more of yourself without lying and hiding anymore (a thing that, in the past, seemed to cause that deep, soul-destroying depression)? And how do I get to do the work I want to do when there seem to be obstacles to allowing a lesbian to succeed?

These are my Christmas thoughts.

I wish you and Rose a wonderful Christmas and a very Happy New Year.

Love,

Dear Lauren,

Here I am again. My new love, Margaret, and I are preparing a dinner for
some of her friends. Margaret is a former
nun who now works at the local Catholic
hospital as an administrator. She is also a
nurse—a very handy person to have around
when I have fallen on the ice, which I did a
couple of days ago, and cannot easily climb
the five flights of stairs to my apartment on
Bleecker Street. I am now set up here with
her until my knee heals.

Tonight's dinner is rather light fare. They
are all former nuns and not extravagant
at all. I think back on our lavish parties

and the amount of food we cooked to share with our friends, and this memory I refuse to share with these women. If I wanted to talk to them about anything at this point, it would be about the impasse I am at with my essay on Bartleby and Jonah as the reluctant prophets.

That topic they would understand. Their lack of hedonistic pleasure interests me. In contrast to their austere ways, where they frown upon or at least never discuss any sort of frivolous experiences. I suppose there is a difference between not indulging and being critical. I should be clearer. The other friends I have are, each in their own way, all for overindulgence in as many ways as possible. But some of the stories they tell of their sexual and drug-related frenzies would not shock these former nuns. They are not prudes or puritanical. I think their minds are focused elsewhere. Honestly, I don't know where. It isn't that they don't enjoy food or life. They do. It's that they are mindful of the waste here, of those in need. I know that makes them sound like a dour, preachy lot. They aren't that either. They are a warm, close-knit circle of friends.

Some days when I am with Margaret and her small cadre—Mary, Irene, and Paul—I feel like an alien. They aren't cold or unwelcoming, but wary. I don't feel included in something; it's as if they are waiting for someone or something here. I don't know what it is. But due to my knee, I decided to spend this New Year's Eve with Margaret. I'm going to enjoy the quiet ringing in of this New Year. Let's hope 1981, with the start of the Reagan presidency, will not be as awful as some fear it will be.

The happiest of New Year's to you, Rose, and Sally. Margaret has promised to go out later and drop this letter in a mailbox for me and go to my apartment to pick up my mail.

Love,

Scags

January 3, 1981

My first letter to you in the New Year. Our letters are crossing in the mail. You asked me what it was like to be in a relationship with a former nun. I hear the little snicker, as you want to say "flying" rather than former nun. Life is cruel and sweet. She is no more like Sally Fields than I am.

Margaret is a truly religious person. Not some saccharine, silly version of one. Sorry to sound so defensive, but I am being changed by our newfound closeness. While I was laid up for a few days taking care of my knee, I could observe her. Watching her on work days was different from how things go when I stay here after our dates on the weekend.

Margaret has a routine during the week when she gets up for work that makes me realize how much I have to learn about her and her religious life now that she and I are growing closer. When Margaret wakes up in the morning and leaves the bed, she's wearing a white, starched cotton gown. In the darkened room, she walks barefoot to an alcove where she has set up an altar. She lights a candle, gets on her knees, bends her head while her long auburn hair rushes down her back, and she prays in the flickering shadows for several minutes.

I hold my breath because I don't want to intrude or distract her. I don't think, though, that I could do that. I have never seen anyone pray. I don't know why people do this or what it is they are saying or to whom. We are so different, Margaret and I, yet I know she has very strong feelings for me and wants to include me in her life.

I think she is being careful and protective of me. She doesn't want to scare me away. It must be difficult for her to find women willing to be a part of her life, especially as it is so focused on prayer, her church, her church friends.

Having me present, though, for these morning prayers doesn't make her self-conscious. After she finishes and blows out the candle, I swear, she has a certain glow to her that is sexy.

After praying, Margaret lets her nightgown fall to the floor. She walks naked to the bed, kisses me, and goes to the bathroom to shower and get ready for work.

She is gloriously beautiful in the early morning. The candlelight continues to glow on her cheeks and in her eyes. As she stands next to me to say good-bye for the day, she shows no weariness or despair. I've never seen anyone look so happy to be going to work. Or maybe she was happy to see me. It is hard to tell. But she kisses me good-bye, tells me to rest and what food there is to eat, then briskly turns away and leaves.

Those couple of days staying with Margaret were a great treat. Her apartment is spacious, old, in a luxurious building right at the foot of Fifth Avenue near Washington Square Park. Her father left it to her. She decided to leave the convent to take care of him when he was dying. I suppose religious orders don't think you should come and go as you please, but I don't know too much about that part of her life yet. I also suspect that Irene and Margaret were once lovers. But again, I don't know for sure.

It's the way they know certain things about each other and laugh at things no one else laughs at. Irene doesn't seem at all jealous of me. So maybe I am wrong or their love affair was over so long ago that Margaret being with me is not a problem for her.

Irene is always very nice to me. Mary and Paul are too. I can feel like a fifth wheel, but that may be my problem and not anything they feel. They are old and constant friends. I am definitely the new kid on the block.

After my days lying around taking care of my bum knee, I wanted to go home. Margaret didn't seem to want me to leave, but for my own sanity, I needed to return to my place. There are always reasons to move on. I needed my own space, and though I felt grateful, I was no longer comfortable being so intimate with Margaret.

It was back to work for me too. And back to my fifth-floor walk-up. I was pleased that I had little pain and could climb the stairs with no difficulty. The combination of my running years and Margaret's expert care helped me recover quickly.

It has been cold and windy here for several days with no letup. This protracted cold reminds me of growing up in Skokie and the frigid winters, where the wind bit right through my clothes. I even got frostbitten playing outside. But here the cold is different. The ocean protects the city, and unlike Lake Michigan, which serves as a magnet for the bitter cold, New York's winter doesn't seem as dangerous.

People here complain about the cold, the snow, but they really have no idea how bad things can get. I jokingly tell them that this blowing snow and shivering cold will serve as a coating of protection against the Reagan presidency about to begin in a few weeks. What shall that bring with it? I dread this change for some reason that I can't even articulate.

I think of my two constant companions, Jonah and Bartleby, and wonder if their reluctance to prophesy and save others is at all related to me, or am I just using their predicaments to justify all the procrastination my life is so full of? You know—finding the real purpose of my life, being more honest about who I am, and so forth. Do you think I can really learn anything from either Jonah or Bartleby, or am I hanging on to them as totems from my past? Can they help me?

I must go now. It is late. I'll drop this in the mailbox on my way to work. I'll remind you, too, that I'm always happy to see your cream-colored envelopes nestling in my mailbox at night when I get home.

Love,

Scags

January 6, 1981

Dear Lauren,

I've been terrified by a dream and need to record it so you can tell me what you think of it. I'm afraid to touch it. Hours have gone by since it shook me awake, and still I feel like I am caught inside it rather than at work writing you this letter.

Let me set the scene for you: This is all in the dream. None of this has happened in real life.

I've had a fight with Margaret, and she kicks me out of her apartment. She is unaware or doesn't care that there is a blizzard choking up everything around us. I put on as many clothes as I can find, some hers and some mine, and leave her. Margaret has become so enraged at me that she has risen up in the bed like a sea dragon, with a large pitchfork she uses to scare me out of her bed and apartment.

I hurry out of her building, past the doorman, who I am ashamed to look at. When I get on the street, the snow falls so fast and is caught within such a surging wind that I can't find my way, though I have taken not more than two steps out the door. I see no markers. Not the Empire State Building to the north nor the World Trade Center to the south. I walk, determined to go somewhere.

My steps in this deep and accumulating snow lead me to a phone booth. I kick away the snow so I can open the door and get inside, removed from the wind and blowing snow. Inside the phone booth, I am warmer, but the snow pelts the glass, and the wind whistles around the four corners like a menacing ghost trying to frighten me to death.

I cannot see the street, the street sign, or the houses. At first, I thought I had gone inside the phone booth to get out of the storm. No, I was there waiting for a phone call.

When the phone rings, I don't need to pick up the receiver. It speaks at me.

"Scags, why aren't you home with Margaret? Why aren't you in her bed?"

I panic. My dream is outing me.

I've felt this fear before. I've felt it many times. It's horrible to me, this panic of being outed and then seeing how someone looks at me with such contempt.

In the dream, the only way I know to deal with it is to go home to Margaret. I push my way out of the phone booth, and then I was no longer dreaming but awake next to Margaret and holding her arm. She was staring at me with concern, wondering what had caused me to grab her. Outside, the storm was as ferocious as it had been in my dream.

Ice beat at the windows, with the wind trying to pry them open. The snow fell in large packages from the sky, bundles of it crashing to the ground. Margaret could have slept through it all, but I tore her from her sleep. I think she can sleep through anything because of her faith, believing God will protect her.

I lied to her and said the storm woke me up and frightened me. She pulled me closer and rubbed my head, and we fell back to sleep.

I don't have any beliefs to comfort me like Margaret has. I see this difference between us and wonder if this relationship has any chance of surviving our early attraction to each other.

When we went to Midnight Mass on Christmas Eve, something I had never done before, I got caught up in the carols, the rituals, and the pageantry, but I was not moved to pray or be glad that Jesus was born.

I may feel from time to time a lack of connection to anything spiritual. As I've written to you, watching Margaret pray at the start of each day is new to me, but I'm not so sure that this way of life Margaret has speaks to me too.

There is a bell tolling inside me. It never stops. I feel it all the time, and I am now thrown off-balance by it. It seems ominous, telling me that I may not be where I should be. I know you used to tell me to listen to these intuitive instincts, but I don't know what this one means at all.

Today is Epiphany. I went to work. Margaret went to church. I am both drawn into Margaret's world and trying not to be. She has never made any requests for me to believe as she does.

When we decorated her Christmas tree, we had fun—she made it fun. There was a magical world created by stringing the lights and watching her hang all the decorations, each with a story about where it came from and what her life had been like then. I know she had a happy childhood, happier than mine. Though her mother died when she was eleven, and that made her relationship with her father strained, which is why she became a nun, I think.

When we finished hanging everything on the tree, we were very close. Margaret made us a light supper, and we sat eating it by the lights on the tree. We ate in silence but were close and could look each other in the eye with no inhibitions. I have never loved like this before. I'm not sure I can continue to love like this.

Please send me your thoughts.

Love,

Scags

January 10, 1981

Dear Lauren,

I wanted to tell you about an urban adventure I had recently. Finding myself locked into the long days of work and socializing, the requirements of my job, the routine was broken the other day when we were visited by two city marshals. I've never been in this situation before, and I had no idea what to do. Being the senior member on the job at that moment—Thom was wisely off raising money from one of our larger donors—it was just me; Will, the office manager; and Sam, the elevator man who hung around in the office after having brought the marshals upstairs.

Sam brought them up on the elevator, which opens right into our reception area. Will and I were eating lunch together there when they walked off the elevator, looking like the G-men in the movies.

I know Will and I looked a bit guilty because Will had found a new sandwich shop and gotten us lunch, courtesy of our petty cash. Fortunately, we had closed up the safe where everything of value is kept moments before these two guys arrived. I think both Will and I must have looked like we had done something wrong, hunched over our focaccia and Brie sandwiches drizzled with pesto, as they walked in carrying official papers demanding payment of outstanding taxes.

Will stood up immediately and took his sandwich to his back office, out of harm's way, but returned immediately. The men in shiny black suits looked around. What could they possibly seize? There was one Selectric typewriter in the room, sitting on a desk, and the phone equipment. We must have looked like a sorry lot. I don't think they knew about my office down the hall, where we stored recording equipment, cameras and projectors, screens, and such. No one said a word while they poked their heads around.

In the course of things, they showed me their badges and handed me papers. Sam stood at the open elevator door in his overalls and bulky sweater, ready to whisk the men away if they proved troublesome.

Will handed me a business card and pointed his face to the phone. No one was saying much because standing in our rather barren offices, it was clear nothing could come close to covering the $1,432.33 we owed in back taxes.

The card Will gave me had a banker's name and number. I went to the phone on the nearest desk—one thing we do have are many phones, all owned by NY Telephone. I dialed the number for a Mr. Mark Marsden, a name that sounds like a banker's, and he answered his phone. When I told him what was going on with the marshals, he told me to tell them that a check had gone out the previous day for that amount. I repeated what Mark Marsden said to the marshals, who had to accept that statement as fact, since there was nothing of any value to seize. I don't think they wanted to carry that Selectric out—it weighs a ton—so they left the papers, said they'd be back if the check didn't arrive the next day, and entered Sam's elevator. Sam followed them in, closing the door and leaving Will and me to finish our sandwiches.

We had barely tucked into them again when the elevator doors sprang open and in strode Thom, looking successful. He seemed totally unconcerned that we had just saved the typewriter from confiscation. He had been at the bank and deposited a large check so taxes and our salaries would be paid.

He went into his office and closed the door. Will and I looked at each other guiltily. I have no idea why we felt we had done something wrong. Maybe it was those sandwiches, paid for with petty cash. And trying to keep those two characters from making off with a typewriter while in the hidden wall safe, we knew there were things no city marshal should see and, down the hall, enough equipment to pay those bills off five times.

Will and I went back to work. Well, Will went back to work. I headed for my office, picked up my things, and headed down the stairs. I knew that Thom's closed door meant I could be on my own. Will never came to my office. I locked everything up as if I expected those marshals would return later on. And I ran down the four flights of stairs as if I had an important date to make. But I had nowhere I had to be and no one I wanted to see.

I headed to the bar, where I met later that night my Artist Squatter friends. But for several hours, I sat in a booth by myself and drank scotch after scotch, trying to shake off the feeling I had escaped from jail.

Normally, I might have gone home to work. Acted like a dedicated worker bee. But I just needed to sit in that dark bar, drink, eat an overcooked cheeseburger and fries, and run up a tab the owner, Froggy (the name had to do with his voice and the way he looked in his paisley shirts, faded and unable to stay tucked in his pants), let us all run up. The thing was, for me, I always had enough money to pay, but I liked being trusted to come back and settle up at the end of the month and get my free cognac.

All we had to do was tip the waitress and bartender.

I got quite drunk. Walking home in the cold after the bar closed woke me up. I got home around three. I had walked straight up Sixth Avenue. The street lights seemed too bright and made the dirty, frozen snow look like I was walking through diamond fields, if such things existed. Taxis were about the only cars traveling up the street, heading away from the desolation of Wall Street at that hour and toward the Port Authority or Penn Station. People from New Jersey or Long Island going home. I couldn't feel the street beneath my feet or the cold air rushing into my lungs. I was an anesthetized drunk who had done nothing wrong but who felt soiled by the events of the day. Don't ask me why.

I took a very long bath when I got home and then got dressed and walked back to the office. I got to the building just as Sam was opening the elevator, turning on the lights, putting his stool back in so he could sit down as he managed the lever that ran the elevator up and down all day long. It was still dark. The heat had not come up yet. I had bought a cup of coffee on the street, from the guy in the cart at the corner of West Broadway and Chambers Street. The strip club across the street was quiet, but had I come one hour earlier, I would have heard the music and seen all the traffic pouring out. This area is close to where Bartleby worked and died.

I know this wasn't such a cheerful letter, but it certainly was more representative of how dissolute my life can be. It feels good to tell you about it.

Love you,

Scags

January 18, 1981

Dear Lauren,

Two more days and the new president gets sworn in. I'm going to get drunk. In the meantime, thank you for your letter and your concern. Don't worry; I don't think I'll become a nun. After all, Margaret left. She left for the public reason that her father was dying and she needed to be home, and then there was the private reason that they had caught her in bed with another nun. Not wanting to make a scene—nuns, I think, don't make scenes but find ways to extricate themselves or be extricated out of these messy situations—they escorted her out the door pretty quickly.

Her father, I think, was pleased to have her home. I don't know if he knew how she left the convent or why. At that point, it probably didn't matter. He was so sick. He had lung cancer and was only alive a few more months. She's an only child too, and he left her quite a fortune. She hadn't grown up here on Fifth Avenue near Washington Square Park but in a house in Queens. Her mother's death when she was young may have also been a reason for her becoming a nun. Death is difficult. Her father sold their big house and moved to the apartment at 1 Fifth Avenue. It's like something out of the movies. Large rooms with high ceilings and molding everywhere that gives you the feeling you are in a castle. I enjoyed staying there when I had injured my knee.

In comparison, my tiny fifth-floor walk-up is in its entirety more the size of a closet in Margaret's bedroom. I don't care. I have the best of both worlds. I like living on Bleecker Street. I can go outside at any time and eat a completely fried breakfast and talk to waitresses who still put their hair into a bouffant and call everyone "deary" whether you are a regular or not. Margaret's building has a fancy restaurant and bar on the ground floor. We never go. We're both more the twenty-four-hour-fried-breakfast type. With large glasses of OJ and lots of hot coffee. Just so you know we can be like that.

If you want to hear news of a wealthy person, I can tell you about Charles's mother, Karen. She calls often and always wants to meet for drinks at the Oyster Bar at Grand Central. She takes the train in from Connecticut. They moved out of Manhattan to have a house with land so their daughter could keep her horses there.

Charles's sister is a lesbian, according to Karen, because she refuses to marry. I don't know if that is a real criterion for being a lesbian, but to Karen, any woman who reaches the age of twenty-six and is unmarried must be a lesbian.

She doesn't think I'm a lesbian, though I am twenty-nine, almost thirty, and unmarried. She thinks of me as Charles's widow. She drinks way too much, which leads her to draw these crazy conclusions about me and everyone in the world. I don't mind because she's so sweet.

The idle rich, these women who are without work but with excessive means, create extraordinary fantasy worlds. She climbs into hers each morning as she gets out of bed, and like her rich negligee, she admires the colors and the textures and spins a web of a story so she can stay entertained and distracted from how miserable she actually is. She knows lots of people and is kind to them in her sad way. Her advertisements for herself consist of hiding within this casement of blonde, almost golden, hair and rich, rich clothes that she then adorns with racks of glittery jewels so that when she wanders the streets of Manhattan, she is a wealthy fortress looking for laughs and a drink.

I've benefited greatly from her generosity. All she asks in return is that I pretend that Charles and I would have had this magnificent marriage. That we would have traveled everywhere and experienced life together. She likes to tell me that grandchildren were not important but only that we were happy together. I think she doesn't like to think about Charles and me having sex. It annoys her because to her, we were this perfect child-couple.

You see? What a dreamer. But I live a bit better than my salary could ever cover because of this fantasy. She knows about the walk-up and has offered to help me find and pay for a better apartment. But I like my little rabbit warren, with its bathtub in the kitchen with a cover I use to eat on. I like my bedroom without any closets but with three walls of book cases and a beautiful stereo sitting prominently on a long plank. I don't require much so long as I can go out to movies, the theater, concerts, buy books and records. Life for me is like a grocery store.

You might wonder what Karen and I talk about. She has that same grocery store attitude toward life, but she sits in the better seats and buys more. She is a keen observer of talent. She can go to a gallery and buy what she likes. I enjoy watching her find enjoyment. Charles was her favorite.

I bite my tongue not to mention Margaret to her. Of course Karen thinks of you as the friend who took care of me during my long period of mourning. I never correct any of this. I just have learned to accept her fantasies.

Yes. There are days when I have trouble being charitable to Karen, when her drinking makes her so sloppy I have to put her in a cab and take her back to this second home they have in Manhattan for these types of occasions. She appreciates me and is so relieved that someone gets her into bed and sits with her to make sure she will be okay. As I pretend to be her daughter, she takes a nap, sleeps off her martinis, and wakes up wanting to play checkers, of all things. We play several games, all of which she wins, and I leave when she's ready to go to sleep.

I appreciate your thoughts about my dream. I agree. I am still having trouble accepting who I am and what I want. Margaret has been very busy lately, going to meetings out of town. I never understand why a hospital administrator has to travel so much. But Margaret isn't one to talk about her job. Unlike me, who has so much anxiety about what I do, she has none.

Maybe it's because she is older and more settled in her life.

I'm tired of the anxiety, though; I'd like to be more steady.

Love to you,

Scags

January 20, 1981

Dear Lauren,

What an extraordinary day. While Reagan was being inaugurated (grrrr) and the hostages in Iran were being set free and flying home, I was in this exclusive bar near Wall Street, eating lunch with the president of the board for the Institute. Why, you might ask?

Because Thom has asked the board to hire me to replace him. He has taken an academic job at the University of Pennsylvania. He told me all of this as we hurried out of the office on our way to meet with the board president. It is good my legs are so long. I had to sprint to keep up with him.

He was in a hurry to drop me off and get to another meeting.

When I say Thom's name, I think of that night he got lost in a thunderstorm on his way to see us. I think of him walking into the house, looking like a bear that had almost drowned. I recall the house's smell of an overcooked dinner combining with his wet clothes and shoes. I remember that big smile of relief he had when he finally sat down in dry clothes at a table full of warm, hearty food. He had had a treacherous drive from Boston to our place. The interview was to have been at three, and here it was, seven, and he would never get back to Manhattan in the storm. I know my six-foot-tall presence at the door had thrown him, and as often as I see that look on a man's face, I am also caught off-guard too. And I remember your exaggerated movements, the slamming of cupboards and the way you banged the ice cubes from the tray to register your annoyance with how Thom seemed to think he would sleep with me.

You were so mad when he left. You were convinced I wanted this job so I could sleep with him. Oh how wrong you were.

I have a feeling Thom thought that we were going to be a couple more because of an image he carries around in his head than because he had any true feelings for me.

As it has turned out so far, he's not that open about anything except as it allows him to further his agenda. In that way, he's pretty consistent. I've never met anyone who wants to talk so much about himself, but the "talk" is about what he wants to get done. On every level, I mean. It becomes evident even when I'm helping him clean up after board meetings. Nothing is put in a place for ease of reach but for some eventual "look" he wants to achieve. We put the wine glasses in a top cabinet because he favors form over function.

That is really the essential Thom. I see a room full of dirty ashtrays and glasses strewn about, and he interprets the mess as some kind of photographic evidence or a data set that will let him rearrange his life to get what he wants, which seems to come down to a look.

This is the inner life of the man who began a think tank to expose and explore the effects of modern advertising on everyday life.

His absolutely only come-on line is this: "Come on, it'll be fun."

My response has been consistent with me wanting to keep my job and my integrity: "Sorry, Thom, I am involved with someone."

While not totally true, I am not sorry; though I am not interested in men, technically I am involved with someone else, and I also tell him, nicely, that I make it a rule not to sleep with anyone I work with.

The part of this wooing of sorts that I hate the most is how it encroaches on my intimate self, making me aware of my body, of how others see it and what it is I want for it. Having to feel the need to defend it has made me conflicted about what it means to live freely with oneself. We all need to feel that we own the area around us so that we can regulate what happens to us.

Thom, as you know, looks like a bear with his big head of hair, full beard, and the tweedy clothes he wears. This bear-like presence turns on some women, but not me. He also uses the think tank as a come-on line with women, but since I work for him, he knows that won't work.

I find it difficult to believe that he wants me to take it over. But there we were, walking toward Wall Street on a particularly cold day in January, as if there was this rush to get this particular chore over with and then we could move on to the more enjoyable parts of the day.

He surprised me though. After this hurried walk and the almost wordless time we spent getting to this old club/bar, he left. He deposited me like he would some sort of escort. And he turned around and walked away. He didn't sit down for a drink and a little chat.

I had met this board president before but never had spent time with him alone and in conversation. The bar was a fusty place. It looked as if it had been around since the mid-1800s, when Bartleby would have been holed up in the office or dying in jail. I sat down in a big red leather chair, sinking in the middle as if too many butts had parked in it for long periods of time.

The chairman, who requested that I call him Roger, was at first flustered. Then I realized, as we drank a couple of cocktails before getting our talk started, that he just had needed some booze to loosen him up. Then he became loquacious in the way older men who like to hear the sound of their own voices hold forth, allowing us mere mortals to know precisely what they think about, which, in Roger's case, was everyone else on the board of trustees.

He wanted me to know what I would be dealing with, as if Thom's selection of me to succeed him was already a done deal. At first I was confused as to how to handle this—should I just let him talk and talk as if there was nothing I needed to add, or should I stop this mercurial flow of words and let him know I was present and had my own ideas and questions?

You know me—I did try for the latter choice, but here is a sample of how that went:

Me: Roger, can we just pause here and look at precisely how you think this transition will be handled? Who will replace me, and how we will find that person?

Roger (looking flustered): Yes, yes, good questions, and I am sure Thom can take care of all of that with you.

Me: Yes, but you, as chairman of the board, should have some ideas. What would you like the Institute to do that maybe up to now Thom hasn't had time to do?

I was really trying to be as diplomatic as possible and also hoping he would ask me in what direction I should be taking this organization.

Roger: My dear, have you had a chance to see what Sonia and her friends have been up to? I don't mean to be a gossip, but there are these clubs in the city, very naughty ones at that, where all kinds of sexual play goes on. Have you been with them? Sonia is a great provocateur and drags people off with her for some whips and boot-licking on the weekends, hiding herself amidst the wildly full-up rooms at the club. Have you been to this club?

He became excited then, recounting the stories he had "heard" about the clubs Sonia took her friends to. Implying, I suppose, that I was not a friend of Sonia's. Sonia is also on the board and has been with the Institute since its founding. She has at times grown impatient with what Thom does or says and calls me up at the office to complain. She is another one who talks nonstop, and when she has finished what she has to say, has to move on to the next thing on her list of to-dos.

For example, recently her anger flared up because Thom had scheduled a meeting of the board at his apartment for five o'clock. This was because he wanted me to be there, and I had theater tickets and could not meet at our regular time of seven. Sonia was (a) trying to find out why the time had been changed (she is highly suspicious whenever anything changes, assuming that it is done to annoy her) and (b) annoyed because a stove was being installed in her apartment that day, and the serviceman might not be finished putting in this superexpensive stove by the time she'd need to leave so she could be at the meeting on time (she will never show up late; if she is going to be late, she doesn't come at all).

The thought of tall, elegant Sonia hanging out at a club where boots are licked and whips are brandished was, I have to say, so ludicrous that my face must have betrayed my incredulity.

Roger: My dear, these are interesting times we live in. People are now allowed to follow their proclivities as if all is accepted. For is it not?

At that point, I knew he wanted me to confess to something—probably that I was a lesbian, because it must have crossed his mind; it sure was apparent to me that he was queer. Drunken Roger was much gayer than sober Roger.

Again, this placed me in an awkward position, because I no more wanted to tell him about my personal life than I wanted to know any more about his. I decided that this was not an interview as you and I think of them—to see if I was ready for this job— but rather one to see if I belonged to the club and could fit in with the wealthy folks who ran the Institute.

I had to ask Roger for some food. At that point, after more than an hour of this gossiping, we had had a lot to drink and I was more hungry than drunk. But there would come that tipping point, I know it well, and I needed to not get to it.

Roger had crossed over it. I saw that he was accustomed to crossing over that line and making a fool of himself or pretending he was doing that. Sometimes, it is not that apparent what people are using alcohol for—to numb themselves, to be more open, to play games . . . and with Roger that afternoon, I was stumped. And hungry.

What is called lunch at this club is this: large slabs of roast beef on large pieces of bread with some kind of potato (my choice) and some kind of vegetable (what they have in the kitchen) and some kind of rich dessert that was some concoction that the chef was proud of having produced. Roger and I had had so much to drink, I could have had a peanut butter sandwich and sobered up a bit.

The food arrived quickly. The staff must use the food to help afford everyone the ability to walk out of their club and get back to whatever life these men lead outside these dark walls.

Roger and I ate in silence from old plates, with silverware that was so heavy it was added work to cut the meat and eat the mashed potatoes. But this heavy food soaked up the liquor nicely, and by the time we finished, both of us were sober.

Roger straightened himself up. All of a sudden, the relaxed and ruddy-faced man sitting across the table from me in his comfortable suit and tie looked judge-like, because that is what he is. As others from the club came to the table to pay their respects, looking me over as if I were a strange fruit left on his table, he announced that our time together had come to an end and he must make his way back to court.

He stood up; he is much shorter than I, and he felt that difference in height visibly. He shook my hand and left. I had no idea what the deal was with paying the check, but it wasn't my concern. I found the rest-room, but the one for women was down in the basement near the kitchen, where I could hear the racket of pans being dumped on the stove and the voices of Hispanics shouting to each other as if they were in their own world, and they were. Women and others were in their own world in this male club.

As I left, I realized that Roger had made no commitment to me, wasn't even interested if I was interested in the job. I couldn't help asking myself the questions he should have asked me and realized that I wasn't ready for this assignment. Thom isn't leaving for another six months, I thought, there's plenty of time to work this out.

Who am I to presume that this is where my life should be leading me? I don't think I can presume a thing right now.

You've seen me in these moments when I am lost and cannot find my way. I am like a painter trying to visualize a canvas of great size before I paint it.

My walk back to work took a detour, and I blame the lunch, all of it, for making me do this. Behind the World Trade Center, on a lonely and mostly empty street, there are a number of places: long rows of small offices filled with numerous businesses that did not get displaced but have been forgotten since the area was destroyed to build the Twin Towers. This area is a no-man's land of lost ideas and lost opportunities.

What still lurk back there are some small businesses with goals for self-improvement. So there are shops that sell a liquid diet guaranteed to help you take off the weight and keep it off. They sign you up for a monthly package of food, delivered to you daily or weekly, and these packages cost so much money that it is only a product the rich can afford. As I wandered along these lost two blocks, which resemble a strip mall more than a part of lower Manhattan, I found a business that spoke to my self-improvement needs. It was not quite a fortune teller but had some of the trappings of that mystical fakery. It was a place you go to be tested for the sort of job you are uniquely qualified to do.

I walked in, picked up one of the clipboards with a pen permanently attached to it, and began filling out the questionnaires.

The questions right at the start seemed randomly to be asking me to decide what I preferred—a long walk in the woods or a day shopping in a department store, a roomful of books or a set of shelves to be put together—all the questions poked me, tested me to see how I made my choices in life, as I interpreted what they were really asking. I was interrupted, though, by the young woman at the reception desk.

Naively, I thought she had someone for me to talk to right away. Clearly I was in need of some kind of occupational counseling and perhaps was also in the wrong business, if what I did could qualify as a business. On thinking that through, as I walked from the back of this overly lit room full of folding chairs, I decided that the Institute tried to be a business in order to deter anyone from taking advantage of it but was actually much more like an ongoing work of art that would never be completed because there was no plan and no form it wanted to take.

All these thoughts cascaded through my mind as I walked to the reception desk. The woman seated behind the large, tall desk had a phone permanently perched on her shoulder. Her head, therefore, was cocked as she studied me walking to the desk.

"I'm sorry, you have to sign in first and pay for these tests. This isn't a free service," she pointed out to me with an accusing stare, as if I were trying to steal something of value.

"Oh, I see," I said, trying to think through how much this was going to cost me. I saw no signs that in any way even hinted at the price for these tests and their interpretation.

She handed me another form to fill out. I walked back to the seat I had chosen in the corner of the room. Right after I had answered all the personal questions about where I lived, for how long, what my phone number was, etc., there was this perplexing question:

Where were you formerly employed?

I walked back up to the receptionist and waited for her to stop talking on the phone, but she didn't stop; she only punched a button, putting on hold whomever she was speaking to, and looked at me with the silent but annoyed "What is it?" emanating from her eyes and eyebrows.

"Excuse me," I said, "but I have a job now. Should I mention that?"

I thought that my current employment was going to skew the results of this test. Rather than wait for me to explain my thinking, the perpetually-on-the-phone receptionist removed the headset and stood up.

She was roughly my height and looked at me as if I were one of the most pathetic people in the world.

"How dare you come in here with a job!" she screamed at me. She walked around the high-top desk and to the chair where I had been filling out the forms. She dived for them and took them back to her desk. Turning to face me as she tore the papers up, she said, "What kind of moron comes into this place and already has a job? What do you do? Are you waiting tables?"

"No, I am an assistant director of a non-profit organization," I told her, and with those words out of my mouth, she began to laugh and hung up the phone. She did that so she could escort me to the door.

"You have the nerve to come in here with that kind of job and take up my time?"

There was no answer to that question. I had everything I walked in with in my hands, and I passed through the doorway back out into the cold of the late-afternoon January day.

When I returned to the office, no one but Will was there, and he was busy bagging all the trash and getting it ready to put on the elevator for when Sam showed up the next time.

I had hoped someone would suggest, "You should be a photographer. There is so much to see and share about what happens in this city."

Instead, I got shown the door.

Reagan, as you know, was sworn in today, and the hostages then were released and made their way out of Tehran. So ends a number of sagas, and so many more begin.

I am full of the despair that drinking too much in the afternoon brings on. This amount of liquor tends to make me unhappy but quite clear headed. I can see so clearly but not with hope in my heart.

I must get to work. It has been such an awful day; work will cure that hurt.

Love,

Scags

January 28, 1981

Dear Lauren,

You are a princess or priceless. What a great present and surprise. The bus tickets arrived in the mail, and I showed them to Margaret, who at first was completely confused. Sometimes, no matter how many times I tell her about a certain person, she seems to draw a complete blank as to who this person is.

But now, she is happy too and looking forward to taking some time away from Manhattan and seeing Vermont. I'm glad that our first trip together is to see you and Rose. I think it is great that it will be the four of us, plus Sally. I expect some awkwardness all around. It is for a very good cause.

I am so glad to be leaving town, as something has changed after that interview. Now when I set out for work, I find myself in this megalomaniacal frenzy. As soon as my feet hit the ground, I am marching, not walking, downtown to get things done!

How odd! I have never been like that. I speak differently, too, to the people I must work with. Will has already called me on it, and he doesn't know what is going on. He has been so sweet and kind to me as I have been finding my way around the office and the neighborhood. He volunteers regularly to buy lunch or to pick up my dry cleaning or to even go to the bank for me to cash my paycheck. He has this solid grounding. The earth wouldn't open beneath his feet. He is married, and they are expecting a baby soon. Will came to the city to become an opera singer; he used to leave the office early to go to his lessons. Lately, though, he stopped all of that. They need the money for the baby. His attitude toward people has not changed as radically as mine.

I expected him to be sad or disappointed, but the baby is, to him, like a big Christmas present that is due this fall. Now, instead of leaving for his voice lessons, he turns on the radio and sings in the back room. When I am up front, near Thom's office, it may be difficult to talk on the phone, but it is a wonderfully human addition to the office setting.

Will also draws pictures of what he thinks his newborn will look like, and he has made little cartoon books to give the child when it is born. He set them up as dialogues between a caricature of himself and the big stomach of his wife, Mona, and he talks to the blob that grows inside her belly. He makes me laugh and think of the work that needs to be done on my essay about my reluctant prophets, Jonah and Bartleby. Jonah being that human inside the belly of the whale.

Maybe that's my hurdle this winter: finishing this long-going, never-ending essay that has been with me for years now. Dragging it out when I began working here may not have been the best idea. I was trying, I think, to find something of myself to bring to the table here and make it fit into the Institute's agenda.

While I have gotten some very interesting and helpful critiques of the essay from my colleagues—Sonia, for example—I have also seen some of the board look at me as if I were crazy for thinking that was the sort of work they had hired me to do.

The interview with Roger might have been the time to clear these things up. Writing about Jonah's refusal to be God's prophet may not have struck my colleagues as the most essential of ideas. Finding a good resolution to the prophet's story as useful for us today while in contradistinction to Bartleby's resignation from the popular culture as a sign of capitalism's fatigue may be somewhat redemptive in their eyes, I do sense a certain change of focus with Thom's departure looming over us all.

My work has now taken on a new importance. Because it is being scrutinized more.

Every day I set out for work in a very different mood. I imagine my day differently. I'm looking forward to telling you more about this in person. I wish I could snap my fingers and that magical long weekend would appear—Valentine's Day and

President's Day all converging. I can't wait to see you.

I can't sleep now. I dream about work and it wakes me up. What if all this mess with the marshals had been my problem? What would I have done? Then I think about the times I have met with some of the members of the board at Thom's house and wonder, just where am I going to have them meet? They can't come to my place on Bleecker Street because it is not big enough, and they won't climb up the five flights of stairs.

I can't have them come to Margaret's apartment because then they would know about that relationship, which I have not yet been brave enough to talk about. Oh, there is so much complexity and so little organizing going on in my mind.

I can, for a moment or two, conjure up a world in which Scags is the right person for this job. She has all the academic credentials, and the board will help her learn how to ask for money from a wide array of people who will be interested in our projects. That is when I get stumped.

I know what I have been working on, and there is general approval for my work. They have been interested in my anticonsumer short pieces, and they are definitely looking forward to the paper on the reluctant prophets.

I wish I could say that that article is going well. I was talking with Sonia the other day about it. She told me how she uses coke to keep her focused. Can you imagine me snorting some coke so that I can keep writing? I'll tell you more about Sonia, but our conversation made it clear to me that there are those who are driven in ways that I am not.

Margaret asked me the other day what made me so interested in this paper and why it is eating me up. She seemed to suggest that I was letting it control my life and that I could handle it in a different way by seeing that whether I "like" the paper or not at this moment, there was a reason I was being called to write it. Those were her words: "Called to write it."

I asked her who would call me to write such a paper.

She and I were sitting at the table after dinner, and I was postponing leaving her apartment to go home to write. She could feel my unwillingness to get to work or to leave, and maybe she wanted me to go. Yet she sat there and we talked more than we have before about my job and what it is I want and whether I will get the promotion, and on and on. I didn't go home as early as I had hoped. But our talk helped me to see some things that I had not been looking at.

For example, I have been dragging this article around with me since I left graduate school. It sat first as a list of ideas, then I read and reread both texts until I could almost recite them from memory, and then I dropped the project again because I was not sure who would be interested in publishing it. Then I used the summary of it in my application to the Institute, and it was one of the items in my package that had interested Thom and helped him to hire me.

I've talked myself into a stupor about setting these ideas aside, picking them back up, telling friends I cannot go out because I have to work on this article, and then, I do nothing. I listen to music, I take a nap, I read a book and eat a big meal that makes me sleepy and lie down and waste the time in these nonproductive ways that don't get me any closer to the finish line.

I can't imagine what it would be like to finally finish this article and have it be one more that has been published and will be recognized as the work that stands for me. That has the name Scags Morgenstern on it and is catalogued along with the other articles I have written.

Margaret asked me also about the original reason I wanted to write about two such seemingly disparate texts. How did I come up with this idea that both Jonah and Bartleby were reluctant prophets, and what did that say about prophecy?

I explained to her that I write in the context of the ways we are pushed as consumers, both consciously and unconsciously, to behave in certain ways and to purchase certain things. That our lives are regulated around holidays when mass consumption is the norm and that from that way of organizing society, we have evolved from a set of disparate communities with individual goals and needs into a society that is pushed toward a conformity of buying habits that threaten to unsettle the entire world. Given the size of the population and its buying power, the government and those who support this kind of mass consumption of things, as well as ideas, are herding us into a one-size-fits-all kind of conformity.

These are not the only things I talk about with my Kultur Klub at work or the Artist Squatters at Magoo's, but this is what drew us together; this is why I am interested in being among them. It is like a religious group or groups that can affirm and teach what is wrong here and to help find solutions for countering these wrongs.

So back to the article and my talk with Margaret: it all became clear to me that Margaret may have a religious calling still in her way of living, but for me, there is no religion other than these ideas that we cannot be shepherded around like sheep unable to disengage from the mainstream's ideas of how to live and what to buy to make that life possible.

I then went home. I decided that even if the paper now did not have the same impetus it had at the start—that I did not see what I was writing as the most insightful ideas in the world about prophecy—at least in my humbler task, it would be easier to finish the damn thing.

With some shame, I walked home. I don't like to admit how much I need to pump myself up to do my work. There have been mornings, more recently now, when I was in need of some kind of "drug" to push me out the door. I used shameless self-aggrandizement. I walked down the streets on my way to work, passing by all the same storefronts, loading docks, fast food restaurants, and warehouses and looked at each of these silent buildings and shouted at them that I was about to be made director. What did they think of that?

The benefit of working in an industrial area is that no one really pays attention to the very few individuals walking down the streets. They might have thought I had just purchased a bottle at the liquor store on West Broadway, or they might have thought I was a high-priced call girl, or they might have not thought a thing because, as I am seeing, women are not as valued as players in this nonprofit world as I had thought they would be.

Sonia told me a very interesting thing the other night. We were helping Thom clean up his apartment after one of our meetings, and she pointed out the obvious—none of the men had stayed to help Thom. They assumed we—or at least I—would be there to put Thom's apartment back in order.

When we left, Sonia and I were parting ways as she walked uptown and I was going downtown, but she pulled my sleeve and said to me, "Don't think that any of them like you. They like you to think that, but if you want anything, you have to be willing to claw your way to get it."

Then she turned away and walked uptown. Her tall, straight back was a bit bent, as she had an accident that caused her back problems. However, you would never see her exhibit any pain or talk about it. She plays these games with them on a set of terms that she has construed on her own or with the force of experience. I can hear that in her comments at our meetings, and certainly I read it in her work.

Pivoting back to me, I didn't know if I could be like Sonia. Snort the coke to make the deadlines, snort the coke to have this growing body of work so that I could not be ignored. By giving herself a name too—her real name is not Sonia Solo but something more pedestrian than that—she has etched her way into peoples' imaginations.

Sonia suggested that I change my name too. I told her I could never give up the Scags name I had given myself. She laughed at me and said not the Scags but the Morgenstern. She suggested I use that one name and no other. Not to link myself with any patriarchal line and certainly not one that recalls a character from a novel of the 1950s.

She then laughed at me and asked how I had chosen a name that was so associated with heroin?

I laughed back. I had never made that connection, but at four or five, who knows what dark forces were playing inside me. To me it was the sound, purely the sound of the name, that gave it force and meaning.

We can talk about all of this and more when we see you. I want you to meet Margaret. I can't quite believe she loves me, but she does.

And I love you,

Scags

February 9, 1981

Dear Lauren,

Thank you for all the wonderful letters you have sent me. I am really looking forward to meeting Rose and to taking Sally out for a walk. Rose sounds fantastic and like someone who you would fall in love with. But as you say, you must be careful both of her, to not overwhelm her with how you feel, and of the world around you, where your relationship is not approved of. Those kids need you, that is true.

I know you never want to leave Vermont, and even more precise that that, you don't want to leave that small corner of it that you have made so cozy for yourself. The preschool is just one function of that world you have created. The children are one part of the population you have organized to be your kingdom, or queendom, the conquest of which was completed years ago.

You realized that living in that same spot where you were born and raised was the only way you felt safe and where you could write the songs you love to sing and where you could build a small empire of children learning how to be kind and loving toward each other—that was what you wanted to do with your life, and it has been fulfilled, day in and day out, for years.

I think I finally understand its magnetic quality for you, why it is where you stay fastened no matter what other pulls there may be from the universe.

I was angry for a time when I first moved here. I walked the streets in the fall, and it was so beautiful. I agree though that it was not as beautiful as it is in Vermont, where people get in their cars and drive hours and hours to look at the leaves changing and to buy maple syrup and take home the last of the summer's harvest.

Those leaf peepers, as they are called, were the bane of our existence in the fall, I remember that. But here in the city, no one comes to look at the leaves. The streets though are pretty lively. And why not? The world is back at work. Everyone with kids is back on that schedule. All the summer plans have been carried out, and the population is ready to dig in and do their part so they can get in the car this summer and go away, or go away each weekend to escape the city heat and smells. Who knew that a city could smell this bad?

With the return of fresher air, though it is still quite polluted, there is also a festival feeling deep inside. The clothing can be more expressive of our wealth and stature. We can purchase things and not resent walking down the streets in the heat with bags on our arms. The jostling of commerce arouses in people a sexual energy to be a part of this place and make it work for them, make them into something more than they were when they arrived.

I wanted to guide you through this labyrinth of activity. Then at night, after a light dinner, take you to a club where we could dance together and not worry for one minute what anyone would think.

That was my fantasy for a number of months until I met Margaret. That you and I would dance every single night until the clubs closed. There are so many of them here, and they are so much fun to go to. I have never danced in my dreams as I did over those first few months when I discovered the clubs. One is called the Barnum, and it is like a circus, a real circus, where above your head with safety netting separating you from the acrobats, very athletic men perform on the trapezes as you and your partner dance to the best disco music around. I went there often on my own for the spectacle of it and for the fun of being in a club meant for people like us and to be able to feel outside what the Kultur Klub or Artists Squatters would be doing that night.

Even as I now recall the story Roger told about the S&M club that Sonia and her friends went to, nothing really compares to this joy. To dance the entire night with people who you feel the closest to even though you really know none of them. I did go home with a couple of different women during that dancing escapade. Having spent hours and hours drinking, dancing, sweating against each other's bodies, it seemed like the perfect end to a fantastic night.

As is obvious, none of those women ended up being interested in having a relationship with me, or I with them. It was the communion of freedom to say, to be, to do as I could not do anywhere else.

The sex was like the icing on the cake. A very tasty icing, a kind of freedom to express myself fully with someone new who I would never meet again, or maybe I would. But to be promiscuous in a world where promiscuity could be the order of the day and night became like a drug to me until I met Margaret.

Meeting her put an end to that kind of casual sex, because even though the thrill of it lasted such a brief time and was not totally extinguished by getting to know Margaret, something else began to emerge in me, which was this love. A different type of love for a woman who was almost like a foreign country to me.

Most women I meet are not as fully formed as Margaret. They are interesting and cute.

I like hanging out with them, which is something I have not done before. When we go out, we are like very good friends who have known each other for a long time even though we only just met dancing the other night. There is an instant rapport. I feel welcomed into a sisterhood. We go to bookstores and movies. We drink coffee long into the night. It's like we are crawling all over each other to share what we already have in common.

Margaret is from another planet. She is stately and grounded. Tall enough for me without any of that kittenish behavior I enjoyed with these other, younger women.

Our time of getting to know each other has been more educational and sexual simultaneously. Yes, in some ways, this period does mirror what went on between Charles and me. I am once again the younger lover wanting to please and learn from the older lover, except the difference in our ages is much greater, and Margaret doesn't need a disciple.

Her life is full up, as some people say. She works hard at the hospital, and she is involved with a large group of former nuns and priests who meet frequently for study. Sometimes when they come to her apartment and we all have dinner together, I feel like I have walked into a sanctuary where I know none of the rules, but they don't care.

I've never been interested in prayer. It gives me a headache. The idea of religion seemed old-fashioned or too hierarchical or male-centered for me to take seriously. Then Margaret entered my life. This stranger who asks me to accompany her to church. Anticipating a headache, I refused to go at first. I then decided to go once. Why? I don't know. I woke up one Sunday morning. The sun was out. It was a beautiful morning for a walk through Greenwich Village, and most people were still asleep. The crisp air popped in my lungs, waking me up, letting me smell the last of the grass and the dying leaves already beginning to form a moldy outerwear. We walked next to each other as if at any moment we might hold hands.

When we arrived at the church, the ushers greeted Margaret with a quick peck on her cheek. She then did take my hand, and we walked over to the side of the church where sunlight streamed in through the windows, warming us up. We got into a pew with another lesbian couple. Behind us sat four gay men quietly reading the bulletin the ushers handed out to each of us.

To me, the idea of prayer disappeared, and I sat bathed in sunlight, surrounded by what I came to call "my people." On this first experience of being in church, which in itself should be marked on calendars as some kind of feast day, I forgot my preconceptions. With that wiping away of those fears and the dread of utter boredom, I opened up a new chapter in my life and now to the story I am telling you.

The organ woke up my whole body, as it felt like I was breathing in Bach. The entire service passed before me like a long performance of a T. S. Elliot poem, except with lots of singing and people performing these slow dances, carrying various "props" for this beautiful performance of what an Episcopal service looks like.

Then in the midst of all this formal movement accompanied by song, it stopped so a priest could stand among us and talk. Give his sermon. At that moment, something inside me was torn open. Sitting in the heat of the sun on an empty stomach, his specific sentences now seem lost in a windswept way, but what remains, because he used this word so often, are these flashing neon signs with the word "LOVE" lit up and floating over us.

How had this happened, I asked, that some strange man in priest's vestments was talking to this church filled with people like me who had to hide who they loved, and all I heard was this constant repetition of that word?

The first time he said it, I blushed. Were priests allowed to talk about love? But then as he continued to mention what had at first seemed unmentionable, my face burned from blushing and these unexpected tears leaked out.

None of this made any sense to me. I couldn't focus on anything other than that word being repeated because in this community, they do believe that God is about love. I can't even find words, now or then, to explain why this idea caused such a visceral pain, why it opened this wound I never knew I had inside me.

I've returned many times with Margaret. Not every Sunday. But I did go with her at Christmastime because she told me there would be plenty of singing. I'm not sure I'm ready for all this speeding toward a spiritual and romantic love. Yet that does seem to be what has been set in motion. I don't even know if I am describing properly what this new chapter in my life is really about.

I mean, for example, do I accompany Margaret to church because I like the music and the singing and being around gay people in a church? All of this is so new. Am I ready for all the consequences of this type of involvement? Or at my age, should I just be looking for fun and dancing and leaving this seriousness for a later period in my life?

As we approach the weekend of our visit, I am full of these questions. No, I haven't spoken to Margaret. She got busy. I've been alone more now than previously, which has me hanging out with my Artist Squatter friends and listening to their stories that remind me how fortunate I am to have a salary and money tucked away.

I understand their angry energy. I watch Bea, the waitress at the bar, working until one in the morning. She never stops moving and takes a lot of crap from all these drunk guys. One night I walked her home. She was sick—as it turned out, she was pregnant. She lives in one tiny room with a bathtub in it in a former bank building. Her apartment was formerly a small office space. The toilet is down the hall, and if I looked into the age of the building, it might have been here when Melville was writing "Bartleby."

We walked up to the fourth floor, where she and many others lived, probably in some quasilegal status that intensifies this restless anger. Bea is certainly angry but not concerned by it. When the fellows tell her to stop being so angry, she yells back—with great irony, I think—"Make me."

I like her gold Converse sneakers and the gold streaks in her hair. She lives her art, which is about gold—the history and its abuses. She never forgets the beauty or the horror of its mining.

My education about art was more focused on, as Bea explains it, being able to tell the difference between a Rembrandt and a Velasquez. Bea intrigues me and baffles me. I see how hard she works, but I'm not sure what she thinks this will lead to.

I have written myself to sleep. I think I fell asleep right on the typewriter. Holding onto it like a pillow and continuing to obsessively pour into it my uncensored thoughts.

Good night, dear Lauren. Knowing I will see you soon has awakened old feelings.

Love,

Scags

February 19, 1981

Dear Lauren,

Have you heard the news today? Oy vey. I've found Margaret. Or she's contacted me.

She was arrested! I know. I am incredulous. She called me from the Tombs. There is such a place. She was arrested in New Jersey with another nun and priest for trespassing on a military base and pouring blood, their own blood, on the planes that carry nuclear warheads.

How is this possible? I came home on Monday afternoon, and within minutes I received a call from her lawyer. A very nice man who is sympathetic to what Margaret and her fellow jailbirds are doing.

He gave me information, which he wisely told me to write down. Papers and accounts Margaret has in her apartment that she needs me to get for her.

You know how angry I was at her for backing out of our weekend away at the last minute. You know that I was so upset, I didn't arrive in the best shape or friendly or even willing to talk.

I have to say that her backing out for this reason, which at that point she couldn't tell me, well, I behaved badly, I know. I apologize, and I also thank you for letting me stay and settle down. It was good to see you, to be with you and Rose and Sally.

I've gone over the past few days. My mind jerks from not wanting to continue this romantic/spiritual journey into the unknowable future to not wanting to break off all relations with her. She made me so angry when she told me at the last moment that she could not go.

I knew she was lying to me. But I never would have guessed that this was what she was lying about.

The FBI has been watching her and now me too. Imagine that. I can't help laughing about it. Me? What would Charles say?

Here I am now, with so many different worries than my job or whether I should stay with Margaret. Of course I should stay with Margaret. She's gone in a very short time from being my lover to becoming my hero.

I saw her first at her lawyer's office. I had delivered the papers she needed. The next day, I went back to his office, and there she was. She looked so tired and hungry. I wanted to take her home, but there were legal things she needed to take care of, and I planned on leaving and coming back for her.

Here's the biggest surprise of all. We had to agree that I become a guardian of her estate. She's going to prison. They're pretty sure that she'll be going away for at least a couple of years. Or more.

I'm still processing that. I don't know how they know that or why she did this if she knew she would be going to prison. She'll be going to a federal prison.

While she's away, I will be in charge of most of her legal and financial affairs. They explained it to me. Personally, it makes it sound like we will be married. I was advised to give up my apartment and move into Margaret's. The list of things that are now changing is endless.

We sat in the lawyer's office. His name is Max Eisen. He's a tiny man with a huge presence. He didn't bat an eye as Margaret held tightly onto my hand throughout this long process of signing things over, giving me responsibilities for her life and its material content. Being in jail had really shaken her up. I've never seen her like this. She acted as if she had been forced into a cell inside herself and been made to lock the door. Taken from one cell, she had retreated into another.

Max's office was small and cramped. Folders sat precariously on cracked leather chairs, a house of cards that required quiet calm so as not to topple it all over, which was how I felt too. Confined and about to fall but trying very hard to hold it all together for Margaret.

Max was the lawyer to go to if you found yourself heading to a federal penitentiary, I was told by Margaret. His filing system didn't inspire confidence in me. Margaret had no awareness of anything; she was a somnambulist. To me, it was only those sparkling blue eyes twinkling from his sharply chiseled and dark-skinned face that let me consider that things might get better.

I received a set of keys for things I had no idea Margaret owned: a house upstate, a garage in Brooklyn that had had a car (now impounded by the Feds), safe deposit boxes, and storage lockers. For a woman who seemed so light and free, now she was revealed as being heavily encumbered with stuff. Lots of stuff, which I now was in charge of.

I still can't believe she'll be going to prison.

We left Max's office. Margaret still clung to me. She said two things as we walked down the hallway in Max's office building.

1. She said, "I need blood." That was why she was so weak.
2. She said, "This is going to be like a marriage. I never got to ask you if you would do all of this for me."

Lauren, I am such a romantic dope, I kissed her right there in the hallway waiting for the elevator. That kiss released some spirit in me, and I knew things I hadn't known before. We were lucky no one saw us.

We got into a cab; I held Margaret's hand and watched the pedestrians struggling against the blowing wind and misty rain. The moisture on the windows refracted the light, causing little points of whiteness to briefly shine onto the window. We creeped uptown toward the hospital. Margaret told me she wasn't eager to see her colleagues. Her protest had made the news briefly here; then, like many important stories, it disappeared. She was treated very well, I'd say admiringly. She truly needed that transfusion too. Like a vampire, she revived.

When we got home, we ate a light dinner and went to bed. Sleep was difficult; we clutched hands, took turns sobbing softly, we whispered partial plans as the thoughts came to us, but it was more like words leaked out, escaping, messages from that deeper stratum where we sleep.

Yet if anything felt like marriage, this approached my fantasy of it. Can you imagine the kind of state we were in that we imagined ourselves married?

As the sun came up, I held Margaret and told her about my parents, Charles, you, and even Aunt Money. I told her about the trust Charles's mother set up for me.

With all these revelations about my life, the curtains I'd installed to keep all relational light from shining in came tumbling off their rods. These huge velvet curtains could not keep out what Margaret had begun asking of me.

Poor Margaret. Was I really the best choice for this exceedingly brave woman?

But we were now joined, and in such a way I had never imagined.

I'm exhausted from telling you this story. Exhausted but inspired. Words have become alphabet soup.

More soon,

Love, Scags, the married lady

February 23, 1981

Dear Lauren,

You're probably just reading that last letter from me and shaking your head with worry. My first piece of advice is, don't worry. What good will that do any of us?

I can't tell this (this being my reason for writing tonight) to Margaret because she is the one I really don't want to worry about anything.

In the midst of all the excitement about Margaret, I forgot to keep my eye on my promotion—how funny is that? I was about to become director of this think tank where I had sought the biggest change in my life, only that was not the change that I actually made.

Today, I woke up and Margaret was already gone. I ran downtown to work. Somehow I made it into the office before anyone else. I went to my own little cubbyhole down the hall and sat at my desk with a large cup of coffee and watched the sun rise onto the beveled sides of the World Trade Towers. Like fingers spreading light on the building, this gloriously sunny day became well lit and warm looking. The light was real, but the warmth was illusionary. It was a bitter cold day, and here where we are so close to the river and the tides from the ocean, it gets raw like in Chicago.

That false warmth perfectly described my day. I kept looking out the window, drinking my coffee from that blue-and-white Greek diner takeout cup, telling myself, I will find out today whether I got the promotion.

The fog I must be walking in never made itself known to me. Perhaps all my sensory systems were on the fritz. I could not have been more frozen from what had to be so blatantly apparent to everyone else. I was going down with no security or safety net.

Why couldn't I see it? Why was this ridiculous "marriage" not waking me up to the consequences of not playing by the rules?

But I walked stupidly right into Sonia's trap, because it was she who had really been the one the board wanted despite the S&M stories Roger peddled to me. She was their darling. Thom was certainly pleased to hand the reins over to her. That's how he put it.

I know I'm telling you this like some jumbled tale. First the ending after having given you my mood. Bad narrative form. But I can't describe it any other way because the other elements are so much more painful. I can watch Thom's toothy smile open up on his face as Roger tells me and the board that Sonia will replace him. That man's lower face plays in my mind like a big silly ad on top of a building in Times Square. The lips pursed together and then the opening of the lips to reveal the white-teeth smile. Pleasure. That's what he felt.

I was bolted to my chair. We sat uncomfortably close together. I heard everyone breathing their own unconscious measure of how thrilling or how frightening these changes became to them.

Funny how that word "bolted" became two-fisted. Bolted to my seat, but I wanted to bolt out the door. I was seeing red, and then they read the indictment against me.

Why didn't I see this coming?

You have no idea what a bolt out of the blue, what a lightning bolt of terror came scorching through me to the point that I smelled sulfur.

When I could finally stop holding myself onto the chair, there in the air was this scroll full of my sins. The sins of omission and commission. I tried to read them carefully. The silence soon ended and Thom said, "We didn't want it to end this way, Scags, but we've unanimously agreed that Sonia should take over the reins. And with all that is going on in your life right now, frankly, none of us are eager to have the FBI sniffing around here. We've no need for wiretaps and such. We do good work here. You've done fine work for us.

"Sometimes there comes a moment when you have to sever ties for the good of the

Institute, no matter how you feel person-ally. I hope you understand."

They all stood up like they knew this ritual by heart. They stood and nervously turned to Sonia first to congratulate her. Her eyes, though, were on me. I did not know if she was afraid I might say some-thing awful about her or if her posture was just that reflexive one, when the leader is assessing possible opposition.

She resembled to me a psychic, those ladies sitting in storefront windows, beckoning us in to see our futures, but who I assume to be hypocrites. The future they see includes their taking of my money. The way Sonia wore her mixture of white silk scarves woven within her heavy chenille scarves made her look like a herald or like one of those figures on a Tarot card. That was how I ended up seeing her—as one of those ladies in the window about to trick me.

That is how Sonia looked. Ready to frighten me. To push me into a future that would not treat me nicely.

I had nothing to say to any of them. The futility fell like a thud at my feet—no illu-sions or prejudices. Just the most powerful feeling of relief from needing to carry this big lie around with me even though at least two others in the room were also carrying that weight. I stepped away, not needing to say anything. I didn't want them to see the surprise I felt at my own release.

Time to move on, I said to myself and left the building, heading to Magoo's. I hoped Bea was there already. I hoped she would be able to hear my story.

Monday's are always strange days at a bar. When I sat down in my corner booth and ordered lunch and a beer, I felt safe. Friends were bound to show up, maybe even Bea. I didn't need to count the money in my wallet. I had a tab.

A few hours later, with me having given up hope of seeing anyone I knew, the Artist Squatters arrived and told me the strangest news. Bea had gone to Hollywood. An art dealer had seen her work, and she was having a solo show. I could not at that moment take in someone else's good news. I was too drunk, too lost in my own big story. Wondering, too, how she could leave me like that.

That, I saw, was the level of my dejection.

I am a child, I have to confess. Confession is good. I'm not so sure that I really know why.

For the first time since I arrived in NYC, I felt that tightening of my intestines. I am drowning in regrets, guilt, sorrows. I've become the widow to my intentions, which now all seem to have died.

I watched my friends sitting together at the big round table shoved into the corner, away from most of what little light there is in the bar. Bobby sketched out their talk as he always does, doodling a scene of tension and caricature, making all participants at the table characters of his own political dramas. Ivana played with her scraggly blonde hair as if there were messages being transmitted through the coils. With her free hand, she wrote singular words down on separate three-by-five index cards. Chester smoked one cigarette after the other, lost in a "thought trip" as he called it. Others came and went. Bobby looked over his shoulder at me, wondering why I didn't join them. I could tell he wondered. He kept a chair next to him empty. That's why I didn't join him.

Months ago, Bobby had one of his plays produced by this hole-in-the-wall theater group with a space near Times Square. He didn't see the irony of his political charade being performed right there in the belly of the beast. He shaved his head to designate himself as author. We sat in the small theater space, which was filled with his friends from the Socialist Worker's Party and the squat where he lived, and listened to the political hollering match between two characters who had no names, just brands, as Bobby called them. The show started at six and was over by seven. After everyone cleared out, Bobby and I headed downtown to this ritzy bar that I never imagined Bobby would want to set foot in. We drank martinis. That, too, was out of character. He helped me home. I'm not a martini drinker. He helped me up the stairs and stayed the night because I think he didn't want to be alone on the night of his Broadway debut. Nothing happened between us. I did not need to explain anything because I passed out.

Bobby woke me up to say good-bye, and I fell back into one of those dreamless sleeps that makes the world disappear. Since that night, Bobby has had a proprietary feeling toward me. I could see it. No, feel it. I feel friendship toward him but nothing more. There was never the possibility of a romantic entanglement.

Now with time to myself and the pressing need to find a way to tell Margaret I was fired, my long siege at Magoo's finally ended when I realized procrastinating was more painful than being honest.

By the time I returned to Margaret's apartment, she was in bed and propped up waiting for me. When I got to the bedroom, after turning out all the lights and shedding my clothes as I made my way to bed, I didn't need a preamble. I plainly said that I lost my job.

The look on her face went from anticipation of good news (my promotion) to one of complete sorrow as she registered my involvement in her case and how my life, too, was being upended. In my anticipation of how difficult it would be for me to face my firing in front of Margaret, I discovered I was much less upset than I thought I was and much less embarrassed. I was just bringing home the news and making myself comfortable in this new "marriage" I was in.

All the new anticipation has to do with what will happen at Margaret's trial, and where is my life leading me to now?

The daily news of our world recedes into a parallel world. There are crises everywhere, and to many, this is the stuff of their connection to the way the world works. Right now, I feel exiled, and I'm learning how to live that kind of life.

Much love,

Scags

March 5, 1981

Dear Lauren,

Yesterday was Ash Wednesday. I don't know if I can even begin to describe how going to church affected me or how I can interpret it for you. I've avoided these church stories. I'm not sure if it's because I'm uncomfortable talking about it or because I just don't know how to tell these stories.

We've been going to church together more regularly. Sometimes just to sit quietly and pray. Prayer is new to me. So are firings, arrests, prison time. Learning to walk in love when I feel that the world may not be the cozy place I had assumed it to be.

Let me alter that statement.

I know the world offers no hope of fulfilling every desire and that luck, birth, smarts, connections bring one closer to the goal than just plain hard work. I also know that, slowly, the tidal wave of all these forces has come trampling down on my former set of goals. I arrived with a list and now live without that list.

Entering the church for Ash Wednesday was like walking into a funeral home. My anticipation of being lost, confused, upset by this first encounter with something unknown to me had me standing closer to Margaret than I normally do. I asked myself what precisely was frightening me. Then I asked God—yes, I did—what was causing me such anxiety. The word "new" flashed before my eyes like a neon sign turned on briefly and then turned off.

Who knew there could be such beauty in the unknown and, in many ways, unwanted?

The service was not long, but of course, it did not totally include me. I am not baptized. I didn't receive communion, and I didn't receive the ashes that everyone who is baptized had placed on their foreheads last night.

I looked at all these people walking back to their pews with ashes blackly marking their foreheads, solemn and in prayer—the weight of Lent now on them, as Margaret says, feeling what these forty days leading up to Easter will entail—and all that was on my mind was how these forty days for Margaret and me were like a completely unscripted play. We are abandoned, I thought. No jobs. No schedule. An appropriate tightening of our belts and a move from my apartment on Bleecker Street into Margaret's on Fifth Avenue. There are things to do, I thought, while all around me, the believers were preparing themselves for the journey Christ took to the crucifixion.

I don't believe. I don't understand. But it is what motivates Margaret, and considering how deeply involved in her world I am now, I guess it should be something I pay greater attention to.

For now, I'm exhausted. All rugs have been pulled out from under me. I don't know if this kind of depression at the end of this long, dark winter is how these Episcopalians experience Lent. But this sadly empty sock puppet feels like taking a forty-night sleep. Let's hope this mood lifts soon.

Love,

Scags

March 8, 1981

Dear Lauren,

An unbelievable turn of events. I'm in Skokie, where winter bleakness speaks the loudest—so gray, so consistently gray everywhere. Pops had a stroke. He's lying in a hospital bed, pretty much gone but kept breathing with the help of a machine. I don't know what to say about this but just wanted you to know. I didn't want to leave Margaret, but I had to get here for Mama. Margaret can't travel out of state. Could any of this be more bizarre?

I'll write more when I know more. Or when I understand more about where all of this is taking me.

Love you,

Scags

Dear Lauren,

I am home and that just has to count as the fastest and most unhappy trip of my life. This isn't a telegram, thank God, so I can write out what happened and then maybe I'll know what actually happened as well. All I carry around in my head are these snapshots of me sitting at Pops's bedside, me at a bagel place meeting by chance an old classmate, me standing with Mama as she both tells me Pops is dead and that I am no longer welcome in her house. Then finally the look on Aunt Money's face as she watches me leave the house. We have all lost so much. It's like a long cycle of loss and recrimination came bubbling to the surface because Mama could not imagine her life as a single woman.

It's always come down to that between us. How dare I do what she was too frightened to do? I never saw these levels of resentment before, and had I, I don't know what I would have done differently. Certainly, I am who I am because I wanted to be myself. Her interpretation of that was that I chose not to be her, which was a huge slap in the face.

I know I'm giving you all this interpretative salad before showing you how it got made. I can't help that right now. I flew home in a silent rage. I felt so justifiably angry; I knew I was right, and Mama was wrong to treat me this way.

Funny things happen on a flight from Chicago to New York. It's a short flight, but I felt airborne long enough to let these pressurized feelings out of my system. It's a kind of miracle to me, flight, like the most ultimate of the trusting and yet mundane acts of modern life. Every day, millions board planes. Without too much thought, I think, to what they are believing in—that the laws of physics are true and that those flying the plane are sane.

I placed myself in the window seat and yanked on that seat belt. I could smell jet fuel and cigarettes. We were flying east at sunset, so the light was behind us; we were flying into the dark, and I took that to be true. I was flying into darkness, a great unknown of so much indeterminacy. I was afraid my anger and fear would affect that plane's navigation.

Pops was dead. Pops is dead. Pops will be dead each day and each night. Yet I say these words and I half expect to find out this is a lie. He's going to pop up from the bed, grab Mama, and dance across the hospital grounds with that crazy, loving smile on his face. Then he'll turn to me, and while no longer able to pick me up, he'll try something crazy like swinging me out as he runs in a circle. Life as I sometimes knew it as a child will be restored, and I'll have some kind of recheck of my life. It will be restored to the way I wanted it to be.

So I flew into the darkening sky with those thoughts in my head. I knew that none of that would happen, but I could accept very little of what was real now. It felt preposterous.

Where to go? What to do?

As you can see, I am totally lost. I don't even know the right questions to ask.

I was just glad to get home, to see Margaret and let her believe briefly that she was to blame for Mama kicking me out of her life before the funeral. It was, for me a relief.

It wasn't that I wanted to be exiled. It was that I couldn't take what death was revealing to me about their lives.

We were never religious. I'm not sure why I assumed that Pops's death would make a difference.

Mama kept talking and talking as if Pops's impending death was a minor scheduling problem, and when he finally decided to die, she for one would be ready to move on and take care of all those things she couldn't do while he was dying.

Why didn't she have something more profound to say about Pops's death? After all these years and emergencies, didn't she see some greater truth to the events leading up to his death? Didn't she wish him some kind of peace or heavenly rest?

It shocked me as I rode back to New York to have witnessed a kind of mundane dismissal of Pops. To have not seen any display of questioning or concern about the repose of his soul, something Margaret had introduced me to by having me with her for funerals where, for the first time in my life, I understood that there were huge mysteries concerning life and death that were not about the romantic tales I read about yearning and loss.

I promise to tell you my stories. There was a need tonight to be with you in this way. Margaret is asleep. I am full of feelings that have the consistency of water. They run through my fingers and roll away, refusing to take a shape and to thus have any names or colors. I cannot live like this for very long but will be able to formulate the stories because they must be told.

I love you,

Scags

March 17, 1981

Dear Lauren,

The news of the day is that we now know Margaret's court date—April 24. Yes, I know, my thirtieth birthday. I never would have expected that to be how I would be celebrating my birthday. Easter falls the week before, so they asked for a date after that. That was the date.

Margaret and I were taking a bath the other night with the bathroom filled with candlelight, just as you and I used to do. She was exhausted and reddening in the water like a lobster being cooked. I watched her let the water relax her and the warmth seep into her, letting her muscles relax and her breath find its natural path into the pit of her being, releasing the stress of this portion of her activism—the waiting to see if she will be in prison and for how long.

Our lives have settled into the organized daily routine of a rare form of unemployment. Neither of us currently is in need of money, and we have pooled resources to make what we have go further.

I sublet my apartment on Bleecker Street. I had no trouble finding a tenant.

We live an ordered life of concern for her partners who are also facing prison, concern for a world that allows such weapons to exist, and concern for our own well-being as caretakers of this highly unusual relationship and experience.

When I think back to just barely two weeks ago and rushing to be with Pops as he faced death, as Mama faced life without Pops and Aunt Money sat helplessly near, not knowing what her role was to be in this new episode, I did not know that I would be the one who was going to be totally transformed.

I sat with Pops most nights, right through to sunrise. I held his hand or dozed off. He breathed mechanically. Nurses walked in, checked things, marked things on his chart, and walked out. He was not really aware of anything. But I felt called to be with him through the night. Then as the sun began to rise, I would leave. I'd kiss his dry forehead, look at his closed eyes, and wish he could see me. Then I'd hurry down to the parking lot as if I had somewhere to go next. One morning as I was getting into Mama's car, I saw two nurses leaving. They were talking and laughing as if this whole night of work had happened to someone else.

Their normal lives made me angry. I sat behind the wheel, wondering what to do. My stomach growled, so I went to a twenty-four-hour deli near Mama's and sat at the counter to have a cup of coffee and a toasted bagel and to nurse the sadness I felt raining down on me and no one else.

When my bagel arrived, saturated with butter, a man seated next to me began talking as if we knew each other. I looked to my side even though all I wanted was the comfort of that bagel and my hot coffee.

I did know him, as it turned out. I had gone to high school with him—Mark, this rather desolate-looking guy who wanted to tell me the intimate details of his life since our graduation from high school.

He had been very popular in high school and must have assumed I'd still be one of those girls who'd be so pleased to have his attention. But I was cross, tired in ways that make me angry, and maybe looking for a fight.

When I told him I had been up all night with Pops in the hospital, he already knew that. When I said I had been up all night and needed to sleep, he became interested.

"I've been up too," he said. I did not reply, because I did not care.

"We could get some sleep together," he said.

At that moment, something began unwinding in me.

"Why would that idea even occur to you?" I asked him and expected him to apologize and leave me alone.

"I know you, Scags. You're off living in New York, but you are all alone just like you were here growing up. Maybe it's time you stopped playing so hard to get."

And so I unwound, because I could only give in to the easiest and thus most honest things to say.

"I'm not alone. I've not been alone since I left Skokie. I have someone in my life now who means a great deal to me, and she and I have a wonderfully complete life."

The look on Mark's face woke me up. The tears began to fall. I threw some money on the counter and left the deli. I drove due east in the blinding early-morning sunlight to the lake. I walked the shore in the bitter cold, on sand that was frozen and covered with snow. I was so alone in that landscape and unwilling to get back in the car despite the wind's threat to remove my breath from my body. Finally, I could no longer feel my hands or feet, so I threw myself toward the parking lot as if I were Dr. Zhivago crossing the tundra. I did laugh at my own melodrama, because I felt free at that moment to go back to Mama's and deal with all that family drama and then pack my bags and leave knowing I had things under control.

I got back to Mama's. Walked in the door and the house smelled different from the moment I took my coat off. There was silence too, like when you can't hear any-thing because the quiet hurts your ears.

I stood in the kitchen a moment before I saw Mama and Aunt Money sitting at the table smoking their cigarettes and drinking large cups of coffee, but mostly Mama had been waiting for me. In the time I had been away from Pops's bedside and had my own coffee and tundra walk, Pops had died, Margaret had called, and somehow Mama got the gist of that relationship, and she had packed my bags and bought a ticket for me to return home.

I felt the wrath like a whirlwind that caught me up, put my coat back on me, saw my packed bags and that look of anxious concern on Money's face. She could not keep her balance against this force Mama had uncorked. I was on that plane, flying into the darkness, and nobody really had time to say any words of comfort or sorrow.

Margaret is becoming depressed. I see the signs and know she will recover, but that will take time. The reasons for it are clear too. We can soak away some stress together, but we cannot change what our reality is. Due to circumstances, love, and trust, we are bound together.

Love,

Scags

March 22, 1981

Dear Lauren,

I appreciate your concern for us. It is really sweet of you to write and to send the homemade biscuits. We enjoyed them. I told Margaret stories of your baking adventures and how I gladly served as your taste tester. What an experience that was. I don't think I've eaten so many cookies since then. No one else bakes for me. The dinner biscuits were delicious. Margaret took a bite and said that they were very light. Surely that is how they were supposed to be.

I also am reminded of our reading group. That wonderful collection of knitters, weavers, potters, and musicians who also liked to read books together. I loved listening to everyone take turns reading. Each voice helped bring out different aspects of the story that I might not have known of before.

Margaret and I have a group of friends from church. A small group of lesbians whose lives have become entwined with ours. We meet after church on Sunday for brunch. It seems to be a tradition among Episcopalians to have coffee together after church and then go to brunch. In this new world I have been thrown into, having these lesbians as friends is helping me to cope with what Margaret and I are facing. But even before we were in this situation, when I was just plain confused about everything happening in my life, I would go to church and pray alone, in a pew, with just me and my fledgling attempts at prayer guiding me.

I've never prayed and never knew why people prayed. It seemed so abstract to me. I brought to it this prejudice that only dusty old nuns and priests like I saw in the movies prayed. Their prayers were all in the service of their own roles in the movies. So prayer seemed self-serving. Like the purpose of all prayer was to make sure the good guy won.

Or the sick kid lived. Or we all were saved from a horrible fate.

But then I moved in with Margaret, who prays no matter how she feels. Imagine that, I said to myself. Someone prays at the start of her day because it makes her feel better, at least that's what I've surmised. Or she prays out of confusion and bad feeling, as I have learned. But for me to pray, it took a day of loss, that ride home when Pops died and I didn't want his death to be obliterated by the drama Mama needed to create.

I prayed that he now find peace. But the odd thing was, I discovered I needed peace, and I knew he would almost automatically be given it.

I took a cab ride home from Newark, the airport being close to where I live, and as I got in the cab with this woman driver, I began to realize I needed help and not Pops. The driver was big, long, and orderly. If a cab can be called organized, hers was. Her voice rolled out of her throat, and I thought maybe she was a singer but with a much less conventional woman's voice. When I asked her if she sang, we were on the highway barreling toward Manhattan with the speed of the jet I had just been on. She turned to look at me as if she needed to justify answering my question. She looked like a man, a woman, old, young, black, white, and Asian. She was everything and so special.

"Deary, don't worry about what I am. No one's ever been able to figure that out." And she laughed and turned her face back to the road without swerving or causing any accidents. We flew into the Holland Tunnel at record speeds and were out of it before I could take a deep enough breath to quiet my nerves about showing up at Margaret's before Pops had been put in the ground.

My prayer was brief. I think that was all I needed. A brief statement of my condition. As this driver lifted us out of the tunnel to land her chariot in the spiral path that releases all travelers from under the river, there I was, not far from Magoo's. With an exhalation I prayed, "Dear Lord, help me through this painful time."

That was it. The driver took me up Sixth Avenue, made a right turn onto Eighth Street, and took another right onto Fifth Avenue. I realized how this small piece of Manhattan had become more familiar to me than the streets I had just walked in Skokie. Those streets, which had helped me think through all my problems growing up and where I had some sort of recollection for each square in the sidewalk—bad bicycle falls, hiding my shame when my body kept changing while telling myself I was not a freak, the jealousy of being poor around rich kids, and then the steeled will to get away from everything that caused me to remember how different I was.

I lived now a totally different life, having thrown off every vestige of cover or disguise I had put on in order to achieve what I thought was important.

When I told that fatuous blowhard, Mark, at the bagel shop that I had a girlfriend, he could not have known that I was outing myself, but I had to. Or maybe Mama found out because of Margaret's call and put the deal together on her own. But however that truth worked its way into the light of day, it has been incredibly uplifting, if I may say that.

My cabbie charioteer winging me to the front of the building, looking at me as if I had formed a bond with her by letting her be the one to pilot me home, awakened in me how truly new my life had become.

It wasn't until later, when I woke up the next morning, that I saw the photo of Margaret and me in the *Post*. I was surprised. Here it was, weeks later, and they had the photo of us leaving the Tombs together, Margaret hanging on to my arm. She was so weak. Having spilled her blood onto that base in protest of the nuclear weapons stored there, she was so tired and depleted. We looked like crazy felons out of some old noir film from the 1950s. Both of us heading out into winter with our heads down to block the wind, Margaret's coat not buttoned and whipping around her.

What a thing to wake up to. Being reminded of that day and how irrevocably, it seems, a life can be changed without warning by the person you then realize has become the most important person in your life.

It is a lifetime ago that I met Margaret at the dance performance at The Joyce and I saw her walk away from me after giving me a look that said we need to know each other. I was intrigued and turned on. I had no idea how to find her, but she found me.

Everything about this relationship has been veering toward the impossible or incredulous since the start. That moment in the lobby of The Joyce, when I watched her walk away and saw how her scarf fell across her shoulders, saw the leather gloves peeking out of her pockets, saw how narrow her shoulders were and how brightly gleaming her auburn curls settled down her back. We never know, do we, why we fall in love or what will come of that love?

I won't lie to you, Lauren. I'm scared and wake up with a stomach full of acid shooting right into my throat. I might as well have moved to a foreign place where no one knows me and I don't speak the language and I don't have any money.

That is what drives me to the church to pray. That is where I have to go because I can't find anyone from either circle of friends here who can see at all what has happened to me.

I need more pockets in me to hold all the various and accumulated woes I have acquired. A dead father. A family exiling me. A lover about to go to prison. No job.

Really, don't you think I am beginning to sound like some *Perils of Pauline* type?

It's as if moving to New York after that comfortable time in Vermont with you has been like a huge bucket of ice water thrown in my face. Something demonic grabbed me as soon as I entered this town. The demon has torn my life apart. I hear it laughing, saying, "Go ahead and find your way out of this mess you have walked into."

Could this mess really be traced back to that moment when I thought Margaret was walking away forever? Could my desire for her have triggered all of this chaos? Am I crazy for thinking that?

I'll stop knocking my head against this wall someday. And making you the sole recipient of my tale.

I love you for being my friend through this. I'm sure your stories are being withheld from me because you are being mindful of mine.

March 26, 1981

Hello Lauren,

Me again with tales of the accepting and the rejecting. I know you have said to just go full throttle—your words, not mine—and get these stories down. Like you said, this is almost a documentary of a very interesting piece of American history that not many Americans are all that aware of.

I do appreciate your understanding and acceptance of what I'm going through. I'm not sure how you feel about my new life or how this journey here has changed every-thing. And I mean everything.

What would I be like if I had never moved here? Moot point now, as I'm here and changed.

I went to Magoo's the other night; I think I tried to tell you about this. I had so much on my mind and thought that if I sat down at the big table with my Artist Squatter friends, I would be able to lose myself in their chatter and become washed of these feelings for a while.

When Bobby saw me come in, he seemed friendly at first, and so did Bea and the others. But then after I had ordered my drink and settled in with them, I realized the terms of our friendship had changed and I had better renegotiate the ways we get on or else move on.

It began because Bobby made some joke about "faggots" and looked at me to see what my reaction was.

"Are you testing me?" I asked him.

Bea stood up for him and said, "We all laughed. Why are you just picking on Bobby?"

"What is that supposed to mean? I thought you had all evolved beyond these hurtful sexist and homophobic jokes."

I looked at Bobby. He picked up my hand and began nuzzling it. I withdrew it quickly from his grasp, and my reaction was so swift, it caught him off guard. I don't know how it happened, but when I pulled my hand away, I hit his nose, which burst with blood, and I mean copious amounts of blood. You would have thought that I had beaten him up the way everyone screamed and pointed fingers at me. All I recall now was the screaming, the large white napkins from the table turning red with blood, and a calm voice in my head saying, "You are not wanted here anymore." Though that could have been Bea.

Whoever said it, they didn't need to repeat it. I stood up and without saying a word, I took a ten-dollar bill out of my pocket and put it on the table and left my sweating drink and walked out of Magoo's. There was no need to look back.

Outside, the nighttime traffic was picking up with the sound of car horns and tires in the slush. I walked not quite home but through the labyrinth of this odd portion of Manhattan where spice warehouses, paper warehouses, printing companies, and new construction make what is an industrial area begin to lose its manufacturing look and take on a ghostly, changing visage. I walked as if I were afraid of ghosts, but I am not. I was more aware of what streetlights were showing of the dirt under the melting snow, the garbage left by waste removal companies that became a new layer of roadway, slippery and glowing in the headlights.

When I opened the door to the church, I was pleasantly surprised that a number of the women Margaret and I had grown close to recently were scattered among the pews at the back of the church. My heated breath caught with the lingering smell of incense. My wish to slip quietly into a pew and review how awful I felt was betrayed by my hacking cough. I was recognized. But no one made a move to disturb my praying.

I had all of a sudden found so much to say to God, as if a long-forgotten drawer in a desk had been opened and out of it came these notes and photos about my life I had kept hidden. But now they could no longer hide.

I began going through them with God, detailing the contents of an inner life that I'd never known I had—all that stuff I'd never wanted to know about myself and how I had chosen to live, that willingness to lie in order to get ahead when I thought of myself as the model citizen who would work tirelessly but who gave up, had given up, on herself when it had been most necessary.

Well, there I was, full of all this vulnerability, complete honesty, crazy-making despair about myself, and our friends became rambunctious, their laughter ricocheting around me, remonstrating me, alerting me that this intense judgment of myself was getting out of control. This spiraling down could not lead to anything good.

These more rational thoughts didn't occur to me until I had gotten up from my knees, gone from the pew to the doorway where my loud friends refused to take their exit, and began to spread my self-righteous anger everywhere, but as I opened my mouth, Regina saw something on me (Bobby's blood) and screamed, "Are you okay?"

I had no idea what she had seen, but her terror for me pulled a patch off my tender skin, and I began to cry for the death of my father, the loss of my family, and that was all I could care about then. There was no Margaret and me. I had no room for that scary prospect.

Regina and Carol took turns holding me. I could tell when Regina held me—her sweater was scratchy. Wool wet from the closeness of my overheated body. When Carol held me, I smelled her body lotion, a sweet flowery smell of a moisturizer I remembered you wearing, Lauren. There was an end to the tears, but it took a bit of time, and they bundled me in my coat and walked me to their apartment in what was now a torrential downpour—early spring opening the skies and making our walk to their apartment on Perry Street a long, wet slog of closeness punctuated by the observance of garbage cans on the street waiting for tomorrow's pickup and the little metal fences surrounding the bases of trees. We had to gracefully clamber our way to the dryness of their apartment while they took care of me, letting me be the carrier of a primal mourning I had held in check since I boarded the plane in Chicago.

We arrived in front of the brownstone they lived in. They had the third floor. The rain had let up. The fierce rainfall had added more misery to the misery I carried around like large stones in my pockets. The added weight of my waterlogged clothing as we all climbed the stairs to the third floor caused me to breathe heavily.

By the time Regina unlocked their apartment door, I had become transformed into a superabsorbent sponge that had soaked up every form of sadness and guilt I could find.

We got inside the door of their apartment when thunder and lightning came into the night sky in quick succession. I could hear their cats frantically racing away in fear of the storm.

I stood in their entryway, dripping water onto a floor mat we three were trying to share. Keeping the wooden floors dry seemed now to be impossible. Carol began undressing, removing layers of wet clothes that smelled like old socks left in a closet. Once she was naked, she carried her pile of clothes to another room—what looked like a bedroom—and within a short time returned in a large bathrobe, the belt tied around her ample middle, carrying two more robes so that Regina and I could also remove our smelly wet clothes.

With all this activity of an unknown nature, the cats came bouncing out to see what we three women were doing with these wet and nasty clothes on this stormy, noisy night.

I stood shivering in their hallway, naked and wet. I looked at the piles of books waiting to go back to the library, the bags of bottles and cans ready for return. The coats, hats, scarves neatly arranged on hooks, and a padded bench sitting under a mirror they must use to look at themselves as they leave the apartment and maybe also revisit when they return to see if they came home okay.

We had been to church and to brunch many times with this couple. I wasn't surprised by their orderliness but more comforted by it than I thought I could be.

Carol pulled the bathrobe's belt tightly around my middle. She then led me by the hand into their living room, where we sat in the dark, drank some brandy, and watched the storm out of their front windows that gave us a view of the sky and the big clouds, which held the lights from the buildings in multiple layers of color. The spectacle reminded me of watching test patterns on TV when we were stoned, except there was more light, color, and the added element of sound.

When Carol interrupted my reverie and asked me if I wanted her to call Margaret, all I could do was nod my head. I wanted to sleep on their couch and to be in someone else's life for a night. In the background, I heard Carol talking to Margaret, giving her the address and telling her to bring dry clothes.

What I really wanted was for her to bring our bed and to let me crawl into it and sleep in Margaret's arms. When we sleep that close, she breathes on my arm, and I feel this regular warm pattern of life. More than that, I try to match my breath to hers so that I can calm down and inhale what she knows about peaceful resistance against a system I have been saying is corrupt.

My writings have only touched on the fringes of the real damage done to us by the twisted messages I have been writing about for my now-defunct job.

I have never been in this imbroglio with myself before. It's comparable to having found myself sitting in a stew pot with the heat on and the ingredients being dumped in, one after another, with the intention being that they get cooked and in some ways blend together while I am supposed to be some part of it and grow with it.

Change of this sort is paralyzing me. So the brandy Regina poured for me was like an elixir meant to soothe those nerves made raw by having to adjust to all this new stimulation, and at the end of the evening I knew why Bartleby would say, "I prefer not."

I prefer not to continue this cascade into religious and political transformation.

Margaret showed up and helped me dress in the mismatched dry clothes she brought. Not even the socks matched, but thankfully the shoes did. Carol and Regina accompanied Margaret and me home. It was as if a knot had been tied and we could not find the way to untie it. Margaret held my hand. Carol and Regina held hands. It seemed to me quite a statement of love for two lesbian couples to walk openly at night without thought of self-censorship. The stew, as you can see, continues to cook.

By the time we arrived at Margaret's lobby, still holding hands and then kissing good night, we had agreed to a joint Easter dinner after church on Sunday at Margaret's along with the others Margaret usually assembled, and it was the fitting ending to a tumultuous day. I am glad to feel loved and be around people who love.

I send you and Rose my love too,

Scags

March 30, 1981

Dear Lauren,

Writing to you with the news on the radio. How is it that someone like Ronald Reagan has his life threatened but does not die? I mean, didn't that seem like exactly the same move Mark David Chapman put on John Lennon? He's not here to live that one out.

It shook me up, to be blunt. It hit something inside me, and I fell down that old mineshaft memory and landed right in my desk in sixth grade when Kennedy was shot. I can't correlate these things well. Trying to move forward, I remember Dr. King being killed and then Robert Kennedy.

As I often wrote, there is something that happens when we watch the unexpected unscripted on television. We might as well be watching a movie in a dark room eating popcorn. The screen in its smallness reduces everything to a distant drama, no longer real, not ever capable of being real. Maybe that's why I prefer the radio. To listen to events that have to be described rather than relying on that screened-in image that should make us all feel as if we were there but somehow distances us and makes its very reality unreal.

So the voices on the radio are somewhat soothing and informative. Reagan has lived; though, as you know, the ship of state was in perilous waters, as Alexander Haig definitely needed a lesson in civics as to who was really in charge—that odious vice president, Bush, the former head of the CIA. I'm sure many people were confused about just what should happen when a president is shot and lives. Who should be in charge until he is ready to assume control again.

The Constitution is very clear. And I'm meditating on this because I received a monkey wrench in the mail today from Aunt Money, who lives on in my mind with that look of utter shock as Mama kicked me out of the house.

Oh, how I hate hypocrisy! In me. In the news. In my family. I think Aunt Money meant well. There probably are some people who feel concern about Reagan. I'm not so sure that Aunt Money really cares about any of this acrimony as much as she cares that Mama and her crazy behavior are now her responsibility. If she had stood up for me when Mama threw me out, maybe I'd feel more sympathy for her. But I've grown weary of worrying about what anyone thinks. I can't change who I am.

Would anyone ever really want me to be different? Even Charles's mother called me to say she thinks I carry around a little bit of Charles's radical ways.

It's all uphill from here on in. I know that now.

You are correct, my dear Lauren; I have exchanged safety and security for a bigger life. And probably everyone believes they can handle it until the facts of that life confront you in the morning after having kept you awake most of the night.

Giving all the love I can to you, Rose, and Sally,

April 3, 1981

Hello Lauren,

Welcome to my world of utter insanity. Margaret fell on the ice the other day. I was with her. She broke nothing. Nothing was bruised. But since then, she hasn't gotten out of bed. She won't answer the phone. She eats if I feed her. She has, too, some very good and faithful friends.

Amazingly to me, they knew what was wrong.

I, however, could not read what she was saying. I don't know her well enough. That is clear. She may be the lover I've been looking for, but we are not long-term lovers or friends. It goes to show you how much of an investment I have to make in order to live up to the trust she placed in me to be a guardian of her life while she is in prison. She believes she will go to prison. I can't believe our justice system will let that happen.

We don't fight about it. I can't bear to place more pain on her shoulders.

Her friends came over today, and they went into the bedroom and prayed with her. They read to her from the Gospel of John. And because this is Lent, the preparations for Jesus's crucifixion and resurrection were on their minds and in the reading.

I confess, I cried. Margaret cried too. She identified with Christ's suffering, the waiting for the proper time, and as she finally spoke and asked her friends to hold her, she said this (or this as best as I can write it down): "No one knows what these actions have cost all of us. We pledged to work together. I have fallen down but will now get back up. My time will come to go to jail. That is not a death sentence, but it is bad enough to rob me of time with all of you and with Scags. I have entrusted her with all I have. Please keep her in your prayers."

I am now going to be silent for a time. We are going away, on retreat for a few days. I will write you when I return.

So much to say, but I must be silent now. Margaret's fear has passed out of our lives.

I love you,

Scags

Dear Lauren,

Yes, a quick trip up north of here along the Hudson to stay at a monastery for the first time. I drove Margaret's well-maintained but rarely driven VW Bug. For the two of us, it was quite comfortable, and because of some forecasts of blizzards, which would have made driving treacherous, we came home a couple of days early.

I stayed in a little monk's cell with a view of the river. At night, I watched the barges being towed up the Hudson. The ice is breaking up, and I could hear the low moaning of it thawing. Large sections, like tectonic plates, wound their way in swirls of grayish frothy water downstream, and in the early mornings, mist rose so thickly I could not see out the windows. The grounds suffer from bad mud. I tried to walk down the hill to the little cove I could see from above, and the first step threatened to remove my foot from my leg. It was fun to feel again, as we often did when we would try to walk through the fields during mud season, this desire of the earth to draw me into her.

With all the drama of this season changing from dark cold to warm muck, the monastery took on this early light resonance as the morning sun filtered through stained glass windows, and the sunsets, still a part of the late afternoon sky, made the darkness slide down the sides of the mountains and burnish everything gold. Until the massive snow clouds began to appear and we had to leave.

Walking into the monastery felt very much like a Dante-esque moment. I wasn't exactly abandoning hope because of my faithless ways, my unconscious and unrepentant ways that had let responsibility slide off my back until the habit of never seeing my culpability in anything led me to this place of no humility and only the proud stance of the critic.

I can write just the bare bones of this conversion, for that was what it was, because one night, lying in that solitary, slim, and short bed, I had a visitor. At first I thought Margaret had entered my room, but the visit was not of the human kind. I do not exaggerate when I say how easy it was to "talk" to this presence. In its voice, which had no discernible gender, I heard answers to questions that had been bottled up inside me.

For example, unknowingly, I had been worried about what had happened to Pops when he died. I heard this visitor say, "He has found more love than he has ever known." In terms of Mama, "She will always find those to care for her."

As to why I was here, what was this all about, the answers seemed both vague and specific: "Do what you know best, and everything else will follow."

I know that it sounds like my fortune cookie at a Chinese restaurant. However, at a Chinese restaurant, the words are not said by some disembodied voice that can then become specific about why any of this matters.

"There is science and art and philosophy and so on. Humans have big minds that need to be put to good use while they are alive. You will always know what to do if you ask me. Remember to ask me."

The room filled with words and light. Time disappeared and when I "woke up" that morning and met with Margaret in the refectory for breakfast, I held her hand, and maintaining our silence, I prayed to remember what I had been told in that little cell of a room with the cross on the wall at the head of my bed protecting me from some kind of evil I was not aware of.

When Margaret and I packed up the car in order to beat the blizzard home, I wanted to tell her what had happened. But I had no words. We drove home practically in silence as the big storm clouds gathered in the northwest. For the first time, Margaret and I were together in silence but not off in different worlds. We were close and calm, relieved of the tensions that had made this trip necessary.

I haven't mentioned anything to her. I can wait. It was so good to have you to tell this part of the story to.

Thank you.

Scags

Hi Lauren,

Just in case you have forgotten, it is ten days until my birthday. Ten days until I become thirty years old and cannot trust myself anymore. Ten days until Margaret's court date, the start of her trial, and the end, it must be said, of what will never be again.

So quickly we have entered Holy Week. I went with Margaret and many of our circle of friends and supporters to church on Palm Sunday. We were a collection of friends, supporters, and co-conspirators. Many heads turned as this large retinue of mostly former priests and nuns entered the church to begin the solemn journey that had taken Christ to Golgotha and that was likely to take Margaret to a federal prison in Maryland.

I doubt most of the parishioners knew what this cadre represented. Margaret had not sought any publicity to try and help her plead her case to the public. That one event, the photo of her with me and her lawyer, Max, leaving after her arraignment, had sucked away any desire to play to an audience. She trusted the "audience," but she did not trust how she would be portrayed. Her energies were being spent on cooking food to leave for me; writing lengthy commentaries about her upcoming trial, as she used these reports as a way to prepare to answer questions; and long walks up and down Fifth Avenue, as if she was memorizing the places where the sidewalk needed repair so she could check it when she returned from prison, occasionally stopping at a local restaurant she had not eaten at in a while, where she'd talk to the cashier and get a cup of coffee to go. These walks happened at all hours of the day or night so she could have a twenty-four-hour memory of the avenue she lived at the foot of.

We stopped often at St. Patrick's Cathedral. She would stride in as if this church were hers. She'd light a candle, kneel, and pray. When she stood up, she'd look up at the blackened ceiling, darkened from all the smoke over the years, and take a deep breath as if she were inhaling memories, not the soot-stained ceiling of this church that had rejected her and the things she did to try and save us all from nuclear annihilation.

Clearly because of your recent experience with the FBI, for which I am deeply sorry, there are many forces at work that want to stop or intimidate those involved in these nuclear weapon protests as well as those associated with them no matter how far removed they may be. Rose and you had good reason to be frightened and angry that they arrived without any warning and interrogated you both. How disturbing and nonsensical. I don't think they really came for you. Margaret and I discussed it. They are building their case but, more to their point, also discouraging people from becoming involved or picking up the flag as Margaret goes away and is unable to protest.

I have been thinking about how it must have felt to find that duo of federal agents with their dour voices standing on the front stoop, arriving at night without even calling you. I'm both glad and frightened that you did not tell him about these letters. I don't think I'm divulging any state secrets here or that there isn't much they haven't learned from tapping our phones.

Mama, too, received a visit from these men representing justice and the law. From what Aunt Money told me, she gave them hell for disturbing a widow in mourning. I swear, Mama has this streak of the dramatic that can spill out like some fog machine hiding all the secrets of the tricks she performs for the adulation of the crowd she imagines before her. They must have been quite perplexed by her. She truly knows nothing and, furthermore, has no interest.

That is the remarkable thing to note about Mama. She spent her married life believing she was Ginger Rogers to Pops's Fred Astaire. It's this movie magic he wanted to star in that drove him to drink, or maybe it was the disappointment that he could never leave the suburbs and become

the singer/dancing man he believed himself
to be. God help us all who live within these
delusions. The rest of us might as well not
exist because we can only be their audience
or the scapegoat for their frustrations.

Not once has Mama called or sent a letter. She is definitely living out her version
of how I have ruined her life. I don't know
what to do because I can't change who I
am. I also can't exchange my commitment
to Margaret for taking care of Mama, who
at this point needs nothing really from me.
I'm sure you understand my dilemma. After
all, we've talked about these potential situations, but I guess we could not have known
they would occur so soon.

And I could not have anticipated on that
first night I met Margaret at The Joyce Theater, as we sat separately experiencing this
remarkable troupe of dancers—Philadanco—
that we would now, every day, be sharing
these moments of anticipating her impris-
onment and what kind of life I will have to
build while I wait for her to come home. How
could one imagine such a life or build it up to
such a reality based on that almost ethereal
moment when I watched her walk away from

me and sensed I would see her again because her disruption of my internal world had caused that metaphorical book to fall off the shelf, and I had caught it and returned it?

Love is not blind. Love is energy. It has made me very hungry to write about all of this. Going to church makes me hungry. Yet it is not food that I crave.

Stay well and keep me in your thoughts. These are difficult and unformed times.

Love,

Scags

April 20, 1981

Dear, dear Lauren,

I am so upset. Yesterday was Easter, and we arrived at the church to find it engulfed in flames. The entire building was burning, and we could see how the whole central part of it was like one giant crater of glowing and smoking piles of wood. "As if the devil were being incinerated," one of the people watching the fire near us said out loud. We heard nonsensical murmurs that the prevalence of homosexuals at the church had caused it to spontaneously combust.

Regina and Carol came away with us when we could no longer bear to watch the flames devour the entire structure. I know

God had nothing to do with this catastrophe, but it felt so wrong—so personal, I should say—that Margaret's last Easter at home should be spent amidst the water and debris of this church she loved so much.

The priests and acolytes wandered around like actors whose entire play has been erased. The bishop arrived and seemed as lost as everyone else. We all surged toward him as he walked amidst the firemen, and none of us knew what to do. This was not in the Book of Common Prayer, I said to myself. There is no rite for what to do when the fires destroy the church.

I am in shock. Margaret returned home yesterday and began arranging her papers again, and we took them to the bank and put them in a security box for safe keeping.

I've sublet my apartment to Bobby, who was in need of a place; I'm a sucker for anyone in need. I want to go there and sprinkle some magic around to keep him safe. I don't think these demons are after Bobby. I must remain in Margaret's apartment while she is away so that her building doesn't try to confiscate it from her. I don't know that I am ready for this address in Manhattan.

I am not ready to let Margaret go yet. I was prepared for the death and resurrection of Christ to be a parable about Margaret. But then I realized you need to go through that scriptural story to experience it. It appears that faith, too, has a component of storytelling.

All those Christians and lapsed Christians and unbaptized Christians watching the fire destroy the church has become a very different parable than the one I expected.

I'm going to put this letter in an envelope, address it, stamp it, and walk up Fifth Avenue with Margaret. We'll turn onto Fourteenth Street and walk across it to Eighth Avenue and turn toward downtown. Along the way we'll see a mailbox and drop your letter off to you. There will be a satisfying shush as it falls on top of the other letters.

The lid of the mailbox closing is always too loud. It sounds too much like a jail cell closing for my tastes right now.

Finally we will stand in front of the charred remains of our church. The bell from the tower fell while we were there yesterday. I'm sure it will still be sitting in the rubble, looking like a lost object, not sure where it belongs but too heavy to move out of the heat and smoke.

More soon and with love,

Scags

Dear Lauren,

What is faith? You asked me that question like faith was something I kept on a shelf in my living room. I don't mean to sound brusque or like I'm mocking you.

But it seems to me now that the bravest thing I can do is live it. Have faith in God—the Father, the Son, and the Holy Spirit. As you've followed me this far, follow me here to see that the only way you'll know I have faith is by the way I live.

I will need to be brave to be baptized at my age. You can't imagine the howling I hear in my head at night when I relive all the choices I've made over the past few months that brought me to this recognition.

I've tried to do everything my way, thinking I was doing it alone.

I wanted to be a rebel or at least be rebellious. But at the same time, I was a hypocrite. I lied to myself about who I was and what I wanted to do with my life.

When I met Thom, he dazzled me with this NYC life. He baited me with how influential I could be and how powerful I would become by my critiques of media and advertising. I readily swallowed the bait.

What I did not ask myself were the two most important questions anyone should ask themselves before embarking on this life.

Let me preface that setup about asking questions by saying I did not know then that God loved me. I'd been hiding from that love, and then once I felt it, I could not say out loud that God loves me.

So the question should have been, what kind of love am I looking for?

Now that I've found the love I'm looking for, it is clearer that I refused to ask or know the question.

Deborah Emin

We aren't free to ask these questions, are we, or to even know these questions exist?

Our families, churches, government, social class do not know who we love or condone it.

But what if no one gave it a thought?

I'm thirty years old now. Imagine that. Somehow, I never imagined turning thirty, not even when I turned twenty-nine. I don't know what this number means.

Today is Margaret's court date. We're going to leave soon for the court house, where a trial will determine if she goes to prison. That seems pretty certain. In the process, maybe some more people will wake up to the dangers of nuclear war.

This becomes a large circle of risk taking. Some risks are big and some not, but the big ones are all the more invisible, like faith. Yet that is what we keep doing—taking risks.

Happy birthday to me. Thank you for the gift of this correspondence and for keeping it between us. Margaret and I are leaving now for court.

Love always,

Scags

Scags has now reached her thirtieth birthday. I could not have written this story about her new life without the help of a lot of people who taught me, encouraged me, or supported me financially to complete this novel.

First in line as a teacher is Fr. Charles McCarron, who baptized me, and Sean Scheller, who lent me books that gave me insights into an earlier time in the Episcopal Church. As always, a number of strong women writers have also been in my mind as I wrote this volume of the Scags series: Kerry Langan, Stacy Parker LeMelle, Liza Charlesworth, and Stephanie Dickinson. Those whose financial support helped keep me focused include Julia Alberino, Linda Gutierez, Susan Wojtasik, and Ellen Leach.

I know from this vantage point—after finishing *Scags at 30* while on a cross-country trip with my silently brave wife, who had to endure my need to finish this book before I could fully participate in this joint venture—that I owe Suzanne Pyrch more than words of thanks.

The new life Scags puts together in this third volume of the Scags series does not come easily. As in all stories of a protagonist trying to find her meaning, this struggle hits her on all three levels of her life—her love life, her work life, and her spiritual life—and it hits her all in one season of the year—winter. In this winter of 1981, from Christmas through Easter, Scags changes in so many ways that I had to make changes to some of the historical facts of this period that I relied on to tell this story. I take full responsibility for all these changes, as I wrote a work of fiction and not a historical document.

With this volume, the Scags series ends the telling of Scags's life as she is living it. The final volume, *Scags at 45*, is told as a memoir. In that form, it is a look back at who she was and what she had done, filling in parts of the story that her contemporaneous storytelling could not have known. Much in the manner of all memoir writers, she attempts to be factually true. However, since her memoir is in fact a novel, truth telling has a very different meaning. There will be no need for fact checkers or lawyers; Oprah will be given no opportunities to chastise me for errors of omission or false statements. The only authorities necessary to pay attention to will be the readers of the final volume of the Scags series. I look forward to sharing with you *Scags at 45*.